TOO MUCH IN COMMON

OTHER BOOKS BY LORIN GRACE

AMERICAN HOMESPUN SERIES
Waking Lucy
Remembering Anna
Reforming Elizabeth
Healing Sarah

ARTISTS & BILLIONAIRES
Mending Fences
Mending Christmas
Mending Walls
Mending Images
Mending Words
Mending Hearts

HASTINGS SECURITY
Not the Bodyguard's Baby
Not the Bodyguard's Widow
Not the Bodyguard's Boss
Not the Bodyguard's Princess
Not the Bodyguard's Bride

MISADVENTURES IN LOVE
Miss Guided
Miss Oriented

SPELLBOUND IN HAWTHORNE
(with Maria Hoagland)
Taste of Memory
Sprinkle of Snow
Hint of Charm
Dash of Destiny
Stir of Wind
Essence of Gravity

BRADFORD BRIDES
Rescuing the Sheriff's Heart
Bending the Blacksmith's Heart
Converting the Preacher's Heart
Healing the Doctor's Heart

HASTINGS LEGACY
Too Much in Common

STAND ALONE TITLES
A Little Clean Fun
Love in the Valley

TOO MUCH IN COMMON

HASTINGS LEGACY #1

LORIN GRACE

CURRANT
CREEK PRESS

one

PALE WINTER SUNLIGHT CAST A shadow at Chris's feet as he stepped out of the rideshare. The light held no warmth to melt the snow mounds at the curb of Two Garden Tower.

"Evening, Mr. Johnson." The doorman's scarf covered half his face. His eyes smiled as he opened the door as he did from noon until early evening each day for the Tower's residents and guests. It would be useless to tell the former bodyguard to stand inside, out of the cold.

Javier sat behind the computer at the entrance desk. Like Chris, he wore a dark suit. He raised his fist for a fist bump. "Hey, you just missed the last roommate in 40A."

"The women you roped me into helping carry couches and boxes for Friday?"

"Yeah. You have a lot in common with her." His roommate grinned as if he'd made some brilliant joke.

Curious, Chris leaned over the counter, hoping to glimpse the new resident's profile. The computer screen only showed the time and the Tower's logo. Well, she wasn't punctual, eliminating one commonality. "Any concern that she is two days later than planned?"

Any irregularity on the secure floors immediately below his principal's penthouse caught Chris's attention. When they helped Simone and Brit move in, the cousins had said they expected the last roommate on Saturday.

Javier glanced around the empty lobby before answering. "No, she works for Legacy Airlines too. Apparently, her flight back to O'Hare turned into two unplanned days at work."

"And you know this how?"

"She came in to have her photo and fingerprint scans today. She talked, I listened." As head of building security, Javier completed residents' background checks from Hastings Security. Still, the woman in question moved on to the same secure floor where Javier and Chris shared an apartment. Chris needed to know at least a few basics. A photo would be helpful, so he wouldn't mistake her for an intruder.

"She didn't do them before they moved in?" Another red flag unfurled in Chris's mind. How did Javier know she wasn't some imposter?

"Couldn't. She was at a funeral. Alan Hastings ran her background and cleared it. Chill. You don't have to worry about everyone in the building. That's my job." Javier logged off and turned the desk back over to a uniformed security guard. Either his roommate had finished his work for the day—unlikely—or he'd heard rumors of the incident already.

"She's on a secure floor below the Ogilvies." Tech mogul, Colin Ogilvie, had designed the building specifically for his family. His inventions ranged from palm reading door knobs to electronic vehicle scanners in the underground parking area. The security team often joked the building was smarter than they were.

Javier followed Chris into the elevator. "Newsflash: everyone is below the penthouse. And a secure floor means Hastings dug so deep they know about the library book fine from kindergarten. Was today that bad?"

Chris waited until the elevator's doors closed to speak. "I guess I'm still in high-alert mode. We had a minor incident at the elementary school where Mrs. Ogilvie spoke today."

"How minor?"

"A non-custodial parent attempted to remove their child from the school. Nothing involving Ogilvies, but the school went into lockdown mode during the assembly. I was involved in the takedown." There was more to the story, but Chris had already rehashed it with the Chicago police and ZoElle Hastings while another team relieved him from duty for the rest of the day. The young school secretary's terrified eyes as the man held the knife to her throat flashed through Chris's mind. If his team hadn't been at the school… Chris pushed the image out of his mind.

"That explains why Mrs. Ogilvie returned late and with a different team. She is almost always home before the children."

"You saw them?"

"Only on the garage security cameras."

"Has anything hit the news yet?" Chris hoped national news would overshadow his afternoon at the school on the local news.

"I wouldn't have needed to follow you on the elevator for details if it had."

"Hastings gave my team an on-call only for the rest of the day." Standard protocol for after action. It would have been longer if deadly force had been involved. "Is your curiosity satisfied?"

"Pretty much. You haven't had forced R&R for a while. Do you know what to do with a night off?"

"I had last Friday off and moved boxes and furniture with you." A half-hearted complaint.

"Are you regretting meeting our new neighbors? You said you wanted a social life."

True. There was friend potential. Chris stared at the elevator's video announcement screen as it changed to show the special events for the week. A second screen reminded those keeping New Year's Resolutions that the smaller in-house gym and pool on the forty-third floor was only for the use of tenants on floors thirty-nine and above. Tenants of lower floors were welcome to use the larger, third-floor facilities.

"Oh, a package came for you. I left it on the kitchen table."

"Wow, that was fast. I ordered new headphones this morning."

The elevator reached the fortieth floor. Chris exited, but Javier pushed the button for the tenth floor and the security offices, leaving Chris alone in the hallway.

Rarely did Chris have the apartment he shared with other bodyguards to himself. He traded his suit for a t-shirt and jeans, sat down with the remote, and pulled up a list of movies he hadn't seen from his streaming service. The chance to watch one without plot spoilers from Javier was too good to pass up. Escaping into a world of superheroes battling over-the-top evil would take his mind off of remembering the look of fear in the school secretary's eyes as she bravely faced down the irate father.

An hour and a half later, Javier came in as the credits rolled. "Don't turn it off. There are two scenes hidden in the credits."

Of course the movie did. The franchise had done the same thing for years. "Thanks."

"Hey, your package is still here."

"Yeah." How had he forgotten his earbuds so quickly? Chris ran his hands down his face. The movie hadn't been enough for him to unwind. Maybe a few laps in the pool would do the trick.

The second credit screen disappeared, and the streaming channel served up new viewing options. Before choosing one, Chris went into the kitchen in search of dinner. He inspected the package with the familiar smile logo. It seemed normal enough until he opened it.

As a pilot, Tian had used hundreds of different showers. They were part of her personal hotel rating system. Nothing could ruin a day like a drizzly showerhead or brighten one like a soap commercial-worthy shower. The multi-function showerhead with bonus rain feature in her new apartment achieved the never-before awarded triple-platinum level of awesomeness. The fact she didn't have to share a bathroom with her roommates made it better. Not that her roommates were slobs—Brit and Simone were the best—but not having to share the shampoo shelf or color code her razor was an amazing luxury. Reluctantly, Tian shut off the shower. If she stayed in any longer, she would relax herself right into a nap. Picking up the unexpected two days of work on her way home from her aunt's funeral put her days behind her unpacking plan.

Faced with a mountain of boxes, Tian threw on her reserve clothes from her pilot's case, a novelty t-shirt featuring a bird relaxing on the tail of an airplane and a pair of yoga pants. She left her hair wrapped in the microfiber turban and searched for the box containing her sheets. A pilot had priorities and her first one was sleep.

A half hour later, her roommates burst through the door.

"You're back!" Brit dropped everything onto the newly made bed and surrounded Tian with the hug she'd needed for days.

"You can thank Simone for the extra two days away." Tian stepped back from the hug. "Did she tell you what she did?"

Simone leaned on the doorjamb. "I did. Brit has already lectured me about it, too. I didn't have a choice. The FO was in the hospital and you were conveniently at Logan Airport."

"You still should have told me I'd be flying with my father before I agreed."

"I was afraid you wouldn't take it if I did. And we needed a First Officer quickly." It was impossible not to forgive Simone's contrite voice.

"Fortunately, Dad knew I'd been at Aunt Ella's funeral, and he didn't ask about Mom or talk about anything family related other than the celebration for the airline's hundredth birthday and the four-generations-of-flyers thing." As a female pilot, Tian had taken more of a spotlight than she'd wanted from last October's article and documentary.

"Legacy Airlines' First Family of Fliers." Brit raised her arm and spoke as if reading the headline off of a marquee. The syndicated article explained how the four founding families of the airlines continued to be the major players in the industry. The Carvers, Hansons, Johnsons, and Pitts were all highlighted. "If that doesn't make the moniker 'Nepotism Air' stick, nothing will."

Tian opened another box. "I'm glad I convinced Dad they needed a photo of all the employees at Legacy who are Great-Grandpa's descendants so you two can have your spotlight. Desk agents and schedulers keep the flyers flying. Dad said they are doing follow-up articles. I specifically mentioned that Simone should be interviewed."

Simone gasped. "You didn't!"

"No, but I wanted to. But I decided your stalker doesn't need any more information. Even if you put me in a cockpit for four hours with Dad, you're still my favorite cousin."

Brit shuffled through the things she'd dropped on the bed. She handed Tian an envelope. "From the county courthouse."

"No package? I got an alert that I had one." Tian placed the order days ago, knowing she'd need the item for her next flight.

Brit shook her head.

Tian turned the envelope over. No yellow forwarding sticker. "Wow. How did they have our new address in the system so fast? You moved in on Friday."

"I didn't bother filing a change of address since we all use virtual mailboxes," said Simone.

Tian opened the envelope. Two words popped off the page. "Jury Duty." She skimmed the letter and then read it again. "Dear Mr. Christian Ray Johnson." The "mister" wasn't surprising. Tian got that more often than she could count. "Ray" should have been spelled R-A-E. Her eyes drifted to the address. "This is for apartment 40H, not 40A."

"Let me see." Brit read over her shoulder. "Oh, wow. I never asked Chris what his full name was."

Simone joined them. "What are the chances?"

"This is the hot guy alert you texted me about?" Tian had received a flurry of texts describing their hot neighbors, Javier and Chris. She'd meet Javier that afternoon in the building security office. Her roommates weren't wrong about the hot part, but he was a bit too flirty for her taste, although his Latino suave was all that.

"Now you have an excuse to meet him," said Brit.

"You should wear your blue sweater. Do you know what box it is in?" Simone ripped the tape off the flaps of the closest unopened box.

"I will not dress up to impress some guy who shares my name to deliver his jury duty letter. It doesn't matter how cute he is. Can you imagine what a nightmare dating someone with my name would be?"

"Worse than Dad's fourth wife wanting to name her twins David and Davy?" Brit couldn't contain the giggle.

"Definitely worse."

"But you go by different names. It isn't like you are Chris and Chris or Chris and Chrissy." Simone pulled Tian's favorite teddy bear out of a box and put it on her pillow.

Tian yanked her turban off and ran her fingers through her still-damp hair. Her grandmother would tell her she wasn't presentable. "I'll take the letter tomorrow."

"Doesn't jury duty have a timed response? You should take it tonight," said Brit.

"Found it!" Simone raised the cobalt blue sweater from the box like a trophy.

Tian wound her hair into a messy bun, using the scrunchy around her wrist to secure it. "I'll take the jury summons over, but I am not dressing up to do it."

"But you can't wear that old shirt..."

"Watch me." The last thing she needed right now was to impress some guy with her name. Tian slipped her feet into a pair of shoes and snatched the envelope off of the bed.

She passed the burnished stainless steel elevator. While her shadow wasn't a reflection, it was enough to cause her to look at her form-fitting yoga pants. Not the best first impression outfit, even if he had the same name. Tian hurried down the hall. With any luck, Chris wouldn't be home.

Javier answered the door.

"Does a Christian Ray Johnson live here?" She held up the envelope.

He opened the door wide and used his thumb to point over his shoulder into the living area.

Brilliant stars and cumulus clouds, a blond man with biceps galore stood near the couch. Standing over an open shipping box, he held a phone to his ear. In his other hand, he twirled her missing order.

Her very private and personal order shouldn't be in the hands of any man.

Tian dropped the letter and grabbed for the pink silicone cup. "That's my menstrual cup."

Two

CHRIS TURNED TO HIS ATTACKER, dropping his phone and the odd item he'd found in the shipping box instead of the earbuds he ordered. He caught the yelling woman's wrists and used her momentum to spin her around and pin her on the couch. She tried to kick him, but his grasp on her wrists prevented her.

Large hazel eyes glared at him. "Let me go, you big—"

Across the room Javier laughed. "She — she—" His roommate's laughter increased with each word he tried to speak. Javier leaned against the wall and waved his arm in meaningless gestures.

A woman attacks him and his roommate laughs? Chris loosened his grip but didn't let go.

The woman attempted another kick at his shin.

Chris moved back, still gripping her wrists. He had no intention of opening himself up to a groin kick. "You need to calm down and explain why you are attacking me in my apartment."

"I'm not attacking you. You're attacking me." She tried to kick him again. "Please tell him, Javier!"

If she knew anything about self-defense, she could have quickly pulled her arms toward her and down, breaking his hold. He used tighter holds when he taught classes for Hastings Security. She could have easily gotten loose.

Supported by the wall, Javier doubled over, his irritating laughter still coming out between gasps. He waved his hand in an all clear.

Chris dropped his grip and stepped away from the woman. "My apologies. I thought you were attacking me."

She looked at Javier, who shook his head, still unable to talk. There was no reason for humor. He pinned someone he obviously should not have, even if she was hurling through the air at him.

The woman pulled the pink silicone bell thingy off the floor. "What are you doing with my menstrual cup?"

Menstrual cup? That could not possibly be what he thought it sounded like. "A what?"

"From the look on your face, you caught what I said. Didn't you read the packaging?"

"There was none. Just a plastic bag with a barcode, and the words 'Mens. Cup.' Which is a terrible abbreviation for something not meant for men."

She winced. "I must have checked the low packaging option."

"Sorry, I had no idea…" Chris remembered his call to the service rep and picked up his phone. The screen showed the call had disconnected.

"Christian Ray Johnson, meet Christian Rae Johnson." Javier wiped his eyes. "I never expected this…" He started laughing again.

"What?" the woman spoke at the same time as Chris.

"Tian… Chris… Honest. I had nothing to do with this…" Javier pointed to the box and the envelope.

Chris looked at the woman. "Do you know what he is talking about?"

"We have nearly identical names." She glared at him. As if it was his fault. She must be at least a year or two younger than his thirty. Clearly, he had the name first. "You opened my package. I was going to feel bad for you since I opened your jury summons. Now, not so much."

The paper she'd dropped. Where was it? The edge peaked out from under the couch. Chris picked up the envelope. "So you are also named Christian Ray Johnson? I've never met someone with my same middle name too."

"I spell Rae with an E." The pinched line of her mouth confirmed she was not a fan of their commonality.

"I wonder how our mail got mixed up?" Chris raised a brow in Javier's direction.

"No, man, not me. One, it is a federal offense to tamper with mail. Two, I wouldn't risk my job for a practical joke—although this one was amazing." Javier wiped a tear from the corner of his eye.

Clearly, his roommate had more explaining to do after he gained control of himself. The situation wasn't funny at all. He'd pinned a stranger on the couch. No matter how many times he replayed the last few minutes the results were the same. The impossible happened. Chris returned his focus to the woman. "Did I hurt you?"

She rubbed her wrist. "I've had worse. You're security too?"

"Yes. Not for the building. Personal security. Which is why when you dove for me..." Chris recalled her words. Menstrual cup. Heat rose in his neck.

"I wasn't reaching for you. You were playing with my...." Her face pinked as she held up the pink silicone object. "Feminine hygiene product."

"The service rep was asking me to describe it. Since I hadn't ordered it, I didn't want to be charged... I saw you coming at me... Um, I owe you lots of apologies. I shouldn't have immobilized you like that." Overreaction of the century. He'd be lucky if she didn't file charges. At least she hadn't pulled the phone from the leg pocket of her nicely fitting yoga pants. Yet. Maybe he could minimize the damage. "I'm really not that guy."

"What guy?"

"The type that uses force to control–or, I mean..." He started over. "I reacted when you dove for me. I wasn't expecting... It isn't your fault. I reacted without thinking. I am so sorry. I just—" Chris waved at the couch. It sure looked like he was that guy. Self-defense wasn't abuse. The word-vomit spewing from his mouth couldn't correct that.

Javier walked over. "I'm sorry too. I should have prevented this. And Chris is right. He isn't abusive. Hastings wouldn't put up with that for a second. Chris had an event-filled day. If I knew you were going to leap across the room at him…"

His roommate wasn't helping. Chris looked her in the eye and put every explanation he could in the two words. "I'm sorry."

"Never lunge at a bodyguard?" The corner of her mouth hitched up in a quarter smile.

He rubbed the back of his neck. "You probably shouldn't lunge at anyone like that. You made yourself vulnerable…" He swallowed and shook his head. "Never mind. This isn't a self-defense class."

"You teach self-defense?"

"Sometimes."

"Oh." She looked in her box. "Well, I should go."

Chris wished he had a reason to ask her to stay and start over. He walked her to the door. "If your name is Christian, how did you shorten it to Tian?" He pronounced it in two syllables, *Ti-ann*, like he'd heard her roommates say.

"I used to go by my full name. Some kid at church was teasing me, singing, 'Onward, Christian Soldiers'. The way he sang it broke the word into an extra third syllable. I liked it, so instead of being a Chris, I became a Ti-an."

"Your birthday isn't October sixth, is it?"

"No, it is in April. Why?"

"Because if we had the same birthday, I don't think we could be friends, but since we don't, maybe we could start over and meet less awkwardly?" Where he could prove to her he was the type of man his mother raised him to be.

Her smile didn't reach her weary eyes, but she extended her hand. "Hi. I'm your new neighbor, Tian."

"Hi. I'm Chris. Would you like to go out for coffee?"

"Maybe some time."

He recognized the brush off for the "no" it was. "See you around?"

"Probably." She waved and walked down the hall.

Chris watched until she turned the hallway corner before shutting the door.

"Now I know why you have no dates. You took down the lady and then asked her out for coffee. You've got no game."

"I wanted to make it up to her."

Javier shook his head. "Coffee is 'I saw your profile online and want to see if you are human.' Not 'I'm sorry, I just scared the life out of you.'"

"She didn't seem scared." As he said that, he remembered her wide eyes—frightened but determined—and how she'd tried to fight back.

"Probably because I was laughing my head off."

"Why didn't you stop me?"

"Why didn't you stop yourself?"

Chris couldn't answer that question. He hadn't analyzed things well. From her wide hazel eyes to the airline t-shirt, he should have realized she wasn't a threat. "Then what, flowers?"

Javier turned and walked away, muttering in Spanish. Chris caught one word—*estúpido*.

"I am not stupid. You could have told me her name and avoided this entire thing!" Chris went into his room and pulled up his relax playlist. Tian had been on the receiving end of too much leftover adrenaline from the day. Normally, he wouldn't have taken down a person Javier let into the apartment without assessing the situation better. Somehow, he needed to make it up to her. He needed ideas. He texted his sister.

> Chris: I made a stupid mistake with a woman I met. How do
>   I apologize?

Janet: How bad?

Chris: I embarrassed us both, and Javier cussed me out
in Spanish.

Janet: Chocolate.

Not helpful. Chocolate and flowers were the usual defaults. Chris scrolled through his phone. There had to be a better way to apologize.

Tian kicked the door shut behind her, not sure who frustrated her more. Chris or herself for flying across the room like a screaming banshee. He hadn't hurt her. His grip had been firm, but not bruising, and her fast landing on the couch was soft. Still, she didn't need an aggressive man in her life. She walked into the living room and dropped the box onto the table hard enough the cup bounced out. "I found my delivery."

Simone picked up the menstrual cup and put it back in the box. "He opened it?"

"Did he know what it was?" asked Brit.

"No." Tian dropped into her favorite chair.

"I would have loved to see that meet cute," said Simone.

"Nothing cute about it. Do you know what happens when you try to grab something out of a bodyguard's hands?"

"He holds it up high enough you can't reach?" guessed Simone.

"No. One moment I'm reaching…" Tian mimed the gesture. "Then suddenly I'm pinned to his couch. With him looming over me, unable to escape."

Brit giggled. "That sounds kind of hot."

"Are you hurt?" asked Simone.

"No. Not hurt. And not hot." Tian replayed the moments in Chris's apartment. Maybe it was a little hot. Those piercing blue eyes definitely were. "He wasn't trying to hurt me, just stop me. It's weird, but he didn't use any extra force. And with those biceps, he definitely could have. Javier was laughing like a hyena the entire time. You'd think he would have told his roommate that we had the same name? I'm more embarrassed than anything. He looked so haunted when he realized what he'd done."

Simone's shoulders relaxed. Too late, Tian realized she should have described the incident differently. Her cousin had been a flight attendant until last year when an aggressive passenger got out of hand, broke her nose, and cut her face. The horrific incident was made even worse when someone posted a viral video. After a stalker with way too many miles started flying on her flights to "protect" her, Simone transferred to pilot scheduling where she was out of the public eye while legal dealt with the fallout. Simone was the main reason they were approved for the high-security apartment.

Brit returned the cup to the box. "He was holding this?"

"Yup. I guess he was trying to describe it to a customer service rep. I'm sure there is a tag somewhere in the box. If I hadn't used the minimal packaging option, he would have known." Tian covered her mouth. "You should have seen his face. He was staring at it so intently, completely puzzled. I'm not sure if it horrified him because I said menstrual cup or because I was trying to grab it out of his hand."

"I read a story online about a little boy who found his mother's cup while she was out of town. The dad didn't realize what it was and the little boy did everything with it. Even took it to school. The teacher called the mom..." Simone laughed.

Brit joined in. "The poor father. Can you imagine what his wife said?"

"According to the article, the mom thought it was funny." Simone reached for her phone as if finding the story again would be possible.

"Can you imagine twenty-five years from now, his parents telling the story at his wedding?" Tian asked. "Little Johnny's favorite toy was..." She let the sentence go unfinished.

"No worse than what I could say at yours—they met over a feminine hygiene—"

"Brit, I told you, nothing will come of it. Even if he is as hot as described in the gazillion texts you sent me this weekend. Just because you have a boyfriend doesn't mean I need one too. Especially one with my name who is potentially violent. When I am ready, I'll be ready." Tian scowled at her half-sister. For a few months, her mom had dated a man with a violent streak. While wimpy wasn't on her ideal guy list, she'd never dated a man she didn't think she could escape from if necessary.

"It's been…" Brit wisely stopped talking before she said how long it had been since Tian's last boyfriend.

"I told you marriage is not for me. I don't want to end up like my mom—or yours, no offense. Yes, there are faithful husbands, but we both have seen so much of the other. I am glad you have a boyfriend. He is one in a million. Please, stop trying to set me up." Tian stood and picked up her box to face the stack of others in her room. Unpacking awaited.

"Are you going to return that?" Brit pointed to the menstrual cup.

"Why? I'll sanitize it." And hope she didn't need it. There wasn't time for a new one to be delivered before her next four-day flight was scheduled to start on Wednesday, unless she switched brands.

"If it was me, every time I used it I'd see him holding it. Add that to period hormones…" Simone fanned herself. Point taken, only Tian was pretty sure it would have the opposite effect.

Tian rolled her eyes and walked into her bedroom. She set the box in her bathroom and returned to her unpacking. Spending half of her month living out of a suitcase, she needed her bedroom to feel like home. She started with the box labeled "bears." Teddy bears were the best type of boyfriends. They never cheated or broke anyone's heart.

Three

Off-duty incident reports were never fun to write up. Chris avoided writing his until Javier pointed out that he would report his unnecessary restraining of Tian if Chris didn't. Hastings Security took their employees' mental health seriously. The way he overreacted needed to be reported, even if it meant another day or two of leave. Five minutes after he hit send, his phone rang. No surprise the name on his screen was Alan Hastings.

"Hello?"

"Rough day?" The answering voice wasn't Alan's but his wife, ZoElle.

"Not really, but I feel pretty dumb."

"Alan wanted me to see if he read this right, but he is too embarrassed." A hint of a smile flavored ZoElle's voice. The mutter in the background must have belonged to Alan.

"If he is beet red, then yes, he read it right. Someone should have given me a heads up about her name. Surely her name wasn't confidential too?" The excuse was lame, likely he still wouldn't have known what the object was, but he might have double-checked the address and seen it wasn't for him before he'd opened it.

"You know our policy. We will pass anything that is a potential threat to the Ogilvie family on. Nothing in Miss Johnson's background nor her roommates' needed to be shared." Alan's voice came through the phone this time.

"Her name. You could have told me her name. Someone had to do a double take. If I had known someone else in the building had my name, I might have checked the address on the box again."

"That isn't the problem. You subdued an unarmed civilian in your own apartment." ZoElle's voice was calmer than her husband's. "She must have been terrified."

"I know. I've been trying to think of a way to apologize. So far, I have come up with a self-defense class, which she needs, but Javier has vetoed. When we helped move them in, she had a box labeled 'stuffed animals.' So I assume she likes them. I can't find a cute one that I can have delivered in less than a week."

"Actually, a self-defense class isn't a bad idea. Those helped me so much," said ZoElle. "I'll authorize that. Sending you an email with a schedule right now. Print off the PDF.

His phone pinged. "You have an email like that at your fingertips?"

ZoElle answered, "Yes, many of our participants receive grants from the Gooding Foundation."

He should have guessed. Likely, the foundation was how the three airline employees could afford a high security apartment. Mrs. Gooding ran a foundation that focused on helping women and men escape dangerous situations. Self-defense, personal security, and cross-country moves when necessary were only part of the services.

"Did you say stuffed animals?" asked Alan.

"Yes." What did Alan know about toys?

"Back when Candace—I mean Mrs. Ogilvie—started visiting children's hospitals, Alex scared some of the young patients, so she ordered a bunch of teddy bears dressed in suits. The bodyguard bears. She may still have some."

She did. Chris had taken a bag of them down to the SUV last week. "Good idea."

"I'm taking you off shift for twenty-four hours. I want you to visit with Dr. Linn before you come back. Records show it has been over six months since your last review with her." Alan issued the order Chris had expected.

"I will. Thank you."

"Good night." The Hastings spoke in unison.

Chris checked the time—not yet nine, his self-imposed cutoff time for nonemergency calls. Mrs. Ogilvie always told him if he needed anything to just ask. He never had. His thumbs hovered over the keyboard on his phone.

> Chris: May I purchase one of the bodyguard teddy bears? I had an incident. It requires an apology.

Three dots appeared on the screen.

> Mrs. Ogilvie: Is everything ok?

> Chris: I need to apologize to someone.

> Mrs. Ogilvie: I sense a story here. . . You can have one. Don't worry about paying me. You know where they are.

> Chris: Thank you. Good night.

> Mrs. Ogilvie: Same.

Chris took the service elevator to the penthouse level. The Ogilvies were not the average principals. Mr. Ogilvie had to be saved from himself more often than not. Walking into walls, doors, and even streets, if he was thinking about some new invention, which he always was. Mrs. Ogilvie was getting better at living with security and the line between friends and protection. The recently adopted children were having more difficulties adjusting to the constant presence of someone in the background.

The backside of the service elevator opened to the suite of rooms for security and the "nannies" who stayed nearby, but not technically in, the Ogilvie's penthouse.

"Johnson, I thought you had the night off." Dana looked up from her e-reader.

"I do. I just need one of the bodyguard bears."

"I didn't think any of the kids at the school saw what happened."

"They didn't."

"Now you have me curious. As guardian of the stuffed animals, I need to know."

If Javier didn't tell the other bodyguards, she'd hear it from someone else. "There was an incident in my apartment involving a woman with my same name and a package. I owe her an apology."

"That's not much to go on. Do I need to ask your roommate to spill the tea?" It took a second to realize Dana was using tea to refer to gossip.

As succinctly as possible, Chris told what happened. His version would be better than Javier's.

Dana covered her mouth to stop her laughter. "You deserve a bear. Don't be too hard on yourself. Bears are in that closet."

Bear in hand, Chris pushed the button to return him to the fortieth floor. A bear and a coupon still seemed lame. Javier scoffed at Chris's idea of chocolate, but according to his sister, chocolate, not diamonds, was a girl's best friend. Stepping back into the elevator, Chris selected two and hoped the small convenience store catered to chocolate emergencies.

Something wasn't right. Tian sat on the bed and closed her eyes, trying to figure out what was wrong. It only took a moment to realize that she was facing south, which meant her headboard was not on the north side of the room. Grandpa said she was a human compass. Her friends and coworkers all thought she was weird, but Tian slept better when her head was north of her feet. She should have noticed before she unpacked. Maybe she was wrong. The compass on her key chain confirmed what her body had been trying to say. They set her room up sideways—a problem she should have realized hours ago.

Tian sat on the floor and put her back to her dresser. Not the fastest way to move it, but the safest. She dug in her feet and pushed back. Her mind spent too much time replaying the encounter with Chris. He hadn't been angry when he subdued her. His anger was later and aimed inwardly, not at her. The lack of detectable anger and his sincerity kept her from calling the police or his boss, and the fact he hadn't left a single bruise. The entire incident was a contradiction of epic proportions. She'd always hated Beauty and the Beast stories. Stockholm syndrome was not romantic. She gave the dresser one last shove, clearing the way to move her bed.

Simone knocked on her door jamb. "You have a visitor." Her voice lowered to a whisper. "A very repentant one."

Tian stood and tugged the t-shirt down. She should have taken Simone's advice and changed before their first meeting. She hadn't expected him to come visit after their disaster of a first meeting. Part of her wanted to make a better second impression.

Chris stood on the far side of the living room with a stuffed bear in one hand and an imported Swiss chocolate bar in the other. Give the man points for finding the way to her heart so quickly. Chocolate was a given. Almost everyone not allergic to chocolate would accept quality candy as an apology. The bear dressed in a suit had a pair of shades covering his eyes and was giving off a bodyguard vibe. Suppressing the smile that came to her lips was not an option. The bear was too cute.

"Hi." She checked her impulse to run across the room to hug the bear.

From her chair by the window, Simone tilted her head and pointed to the couch.

Tian took the hint. "Would you like to have a seat?"

He didn't move from where he stood. "I just came to give you these. And tell you again how sorry I am."

Brit slipped into the other chair, leaving only the couch for Chris and Tian. Her roommates were making the entire apology thing more difficult than it needed to be. Apologies don't require audiences.

"Wherever did you find the adorable bear?" Tian sat on the arm of the couch.

Glancing at each of the three women, Chris sat on the far end of the couch. He held out the bear and the chocolate. "Mrs. Ogilvie keeps a supply of bodyguard bears for when she visits children's hospitals."

"Candace Ogilvie? The artist?" asked Brit. "I love her podcasts. When she talks about her mom I know just how she feels since my mom died of breast cancer too, and I love her perspectives on everything."

Still holding his offerings, Chris shifted in his seat. "Umm, yes."

Tian slid off the couch arm onto the cushion and took the items from Chris. The bear was softer than it looked. Rather than wool, the suit was a huggable fleece. "You didn't need to go to all the trouble."

"I did. Subduing you was inexcusable. I overreacted because I wasn't paying attention to the situation. If you would like to file a complaint to either Hastings Security or the police, I would understand." He took a folded paper from his pocket. "Hastings's contact number is on here. Ask to speak to ZoElle—"

Simone interrupted with a loud gasp. "You were at the school today, weren't you?"

Chris looked at his hands for a long moment. "I am not in a position to confirm that."

Tian's focus bounced between her roommate and the man sitting next to her.

"You didn't ask what school…you must know what I am talking about. You are the 'unidentified citizen' aren't you? Mrs. Ogilvie was at that school, and you are her bodyguard." Simone pointed at Chris.

The bodyguard looked her in the eye. "I am sure whatever you heard was exaggerated."

"Wait, what? The guy with the knife?" asked Brit. "So awesome that you saved all those kids."

"Children were never in any danger." Chris's clarification confirmed Simone was correct.

Tian waved her hand. "Can someone please fill me in?"

Simone leaned forward. "Mrs. Ogilvie was doing an assembly at an elementary school. A guy shows up demanding his kid, waving a knife, and threatening people in the office. He grabs one secretary and a 'private citizen'"—Simone uses air quotes—"disarms him and holds the guy for the police. It happened so fast the students didn't know anything had happened."

Tian studied Chris. "That was you, wasn't it?"

He slowly nodded. "I was at the right place at the right time. That is why I was home early today. Please don't put my name on social media or anything. I slipped when I said Mrs. Ogilvie's name, although living in the building, you'd probably notice I spend most of my time near the Ogilvie family."

"Were you decompressing when I came to your apartment?" Tian understood the aftermath of an adrenaline rush all too well. The good ones like a perfect landing on a windy day. Or the not so good ones between lightening strikes.

"Yes."

She unfolded the paper. "Advanced self-defense class?"

"Your first instinct was to kick me. If you had pulled your arms straight down, you would have been free of me. I had you in an awkward hold."

"Do you teach this class?"

"No. Either current or former female bodyguards teach all the classes for women's self-defense. Occasionally I play the role of live test dummy."

"Why the advanced class?"

Simone answered, "This lease came with the basic class for all of us. I'm sure I emailed you about it."

"You email me about a lot of things. I guess I wasn't paying attention."

"I knew it." Simone's triumphant tone was completely unnecessary. A dozen emails about the new apartment remained ignored in her inbox, knowing Simone would recap in another one.

Chris stood. "I should go. If there is anything I can ever do for you…"

"Actually, if you have a minute, I was rearranging my furniture, and it would go faster with"—Tian needed another word other than the biceps she was staring at—"an extra set of hands."

"Sure."

Tian walked to her room with him following. Maybe she had suffered a concussion. She never invited guys into her room.

Tian set his gifts on the dresser, which was on a different wall than it had been Friday night. The trail left in the carpet showed where it had been pushed. "Did you move that yourself?"

"Yes."

Chris pursed his lips. It wasn't his place to lecture her on back injuries.

Simone and Brit hovered at the door. Obviously, they had no intention of leaving their roommate alone with him. Good for them.

"Where do you want the bed?" he asked.

"North." Tian pointed to the center of the recently vacated wall.

The bed sat on a wooden frame that looked as if it had seen better days. "I think we should take the mattress off to move the frame."

Tian pulled off the comforter. "That was my plan. I only wished I hadn't made the bed before I realized it was on the east wall."

That was the second time she referred, correctly, to compass directions. Few people used them.

Simone helped Tian remove the sheet. "It is so weird that you know which way is north when you are inside of a room."

"It's her stupid-human trick. Dad says she is better than GPS." Brit took the pillows out of the room. "I didn't inherit that gene. I get lost if someone tells me to turn right at the corner."

"You are sisters?" Avoiding any comment about women and directions seemed safest.

"Half-sisters. Our father is the cliché airline pilot with a woman in every city." Venom laced Tian's words.

Perhaps comments or jokes about directions would have been a better question. Chris took hold of the mattress corner nearest him. "If we lean the mattress against the bathroom door, it should be out of the way."

Tian and Simone lifted the other side, and Brit stepped out of his way. One of the ancient support slats slid sideways and fell to the floor, affirming Chris's thoughts about moving the frame without the mattress on it. "Will the frame hold together when we rotate it?"

"It should. The slats may fall out." Tian kicked the fallen slat in the direction the bed would move.

"You could screw them in."

"The bed is an antique. My great grandfather made it for my grandma. I'm afraid I'll ruin it."

With the four of them, it only took a minute to move the frame into the new position, fix the support slats, and replace the mattress.

"Thanks. You saved me a good hour of moving furniture."

Brit put her hand on her hip. "You could have asked us for help."

Tian shrugged. "You were busy."

Chris pointed to the nightstand. "Where do you want this?"

"Over on this side of the bed, if it isn't too much of a problem."

Made of the same wood as the bed, the nightstand was heavier than he expected. The eyes of all three women followed him. He hadn't meant to show off, but he wasn't naïve enough to think that it was anything other than his biceps that impressed them. He placed the piece next to the head of the bed.

Chris straightened and turned. All three women averted their gazes to look in random directions. They had been staring. His ego smiled, but he kept his bodyguard's passive face on. "Anything else?"

"No, thank you." Tian walked out of the room, a silent invitation for him to leave too. Brit and Simone stayed in the bedroom.

Now that he was alone with Tian, Chris wasn't sure if he should apologize again or not. Near the door, Tian turned to face him. "Thank you for the help, the bear, and the apology."

"Next time I get mail, I'm going to double check thst it is for me."

"Ditto." She stuck out her hand. "Friends?"

Chris completed the handshake. Her grip was firmer than he expected, and her hand fit nicely in his. He held her a half beat too long. "Friends? With names like ours, we'd better be."

"True. It is safer that way."

"I am sorry. I—"

"You don't need to keep apologizing." She laid her hand on his forearm.

Every nerve ending, suddenly aware of her touch, waited for his next move. Murphy's law hated him. No way could he ever act on the attraction he felt. They had the same name. And the way they met would keep him in the friend zone forever. He moved from her touch and put his hand on the doorknob. "Good night, Tian."

Four

Tian dropped the last of the flattened boxes off in the building recycling center and went in search of the workout room Javier had told her about. There was a gym and pool on the lower floors; however, since they were in the higher security section, she could access the smaller weight room and lap pool on the 43rd floor. As she assumed, the room was mostly empty at ten in the morning. In the far corner, a woman ran on a treadmill and a man swam laps in the three-lane pool visible through a glass wall.

Tian chose a treadmill near the center of the wall and brought up the screen. So many choices. Unsure how the high-end machine would respond, Tian chose a run program with a medium difficulty, slipped in her earbuds and ran.

The treadmill screen displayed a view of a mountain trail. Nice. If every hotel she stayed in had a treadmill like this one she would have fewer excuses not to exercise. A mile into her run, Tian noticed the view of the pool was more interesting than the exercise screen. The male swimmer switched from freestyle to butterfly stroke and stole her breath. Sensing movement to her side, Tian glanced over to see the woman who had been running earlier, drinking from her water bottle also taking in the view through the window separating them from the pool.

The woman said something. Tian pulled out her earbud. "What?"

"I said, I'm getting a second workout watching him."

"Does he usually exercise at this time?"

The woman shook her head. "No, usually I'm alone up here. By the way, I'm Dana."

"I'm Tian. I moved in yesterday."

"Welcome to the Tower." Dana lifted her water bottle in a type of salute. "I'd stay and enjoy the view, but I need to go to work. See you around."

"Bye." Tian slipped her earbud back in. Her twenty-minute run program entered the cool-down phase. The swimmer also seemed to slow and switched to a backstroke. The treadmill signaled the end of her workout. Next time, she'd try something more challenging. If she woke up a half hour earlier tomorrow, she could fit in a workout before leaving for her morning flight.

She stretched out in the mat area to her right. From her mountain pose, she watched the man push up out of the pool. Good thing she had both feet firmly planted on the ground. Each clearly defined muscle moved smoothly along his back as he crossed to his towel and pulled off his swim cap. The purpose of yoga wasn't to speed up the heart. Tian moved her focus to the clear glass in front of her and lifted her foot for the tree pose.

She closed her eyes and breathed out through her nose. Someone knocked on the glass. She opened her eyes to see Chris's smiling face from the poolside. Up close, his pectoral muscles were—

Tian lost her balance, falling out of her pose.

"I didn't mean to startle you." Chris entered the gym from a glass door she hadn't noticed, a towel over his shoulder and another around his waist.

"I didn't mean to stare." Lie. Yes, she did. "I mean—Hi, How are you?"

"Fine. I rarely have the pool to myself. It's nice not having to worry about splashing anyone." The twinkle in his eye let her know he knew she'd watched him swim.

Tian reached for her water bottle. Anything to keep her from rudely staring at him. "It is a great gym."

"Yup, and I am dripping… See you later." Chris entered the dressing room, and Tian let out a breath before returning to her yoga pose. Her heart and mind refused to join her body in finding a peaceful balance after watching him swim and seeing the muscles when he moved her nightstand last night. Tian moved into the last of her relaxing poses. The Savasana put her laying on her back, eyes closed. As she heard someone enter the room, she rolled up into a sitting position. As she'd hoped, it was Chris.

"Do you have a minute?" Tian stood.

He checked his watch. "Yes."

"Last night in your apartment. You could have hurt me, but you didn't." Tian held up her unbruised wrists. "How? Why?"

He rubbed the back of his neck. "I was only trying to stop you from hurting me, not capture a felon. I only used the force necessary. It was pretty subconscious, I think."

"So you don't have an explanation?"

"Training maybe? Either that or Javier's laughing."

"Last night you said I could have easily gotten out of the hold. How?"

Chris looked around. "I'll show you. We can use that bench. I'll be you."

He sat on the bench and crossed his arms over his chest the way her arms had been when she was pinned. "Pretend you're me and grab my wrists."

Tian leaned over him and grabbed his wrists.

"A little closer. I promise not to hurt you."

Not physically, but their position had her insides bouncing around as if they had never heard of being calm.

"Move your hands a little lower."

She did.

"See how my arms are crossed? It wasn't the most ideal grip for me. I'll show you why. I'm going to move my arms slowly. Let go when you feel the pressure." Chris rotated his arms down as he did, his arms uncrossed and hers crossed and rotated.

Her grip became hard to hold and with her arms crossed in this position, her arms pressed against each other. Tian let go. "Easy enough for you. My muscles don't compare."

Chris shook his head. "You don't need to be stronger than me. Just fast. The faster you do it, the more I am caught off guard. Let's switch and I'll prove it."

Tian sat where Chris had and crossed her arms.

He gripped her wrists as he had in his apartment. His hold was firm, but not painful. "You okay?"

"I'm good." Too good. He smelled of soap and a hint of something that pulled on her memory from last night. A cologne she couldn't place.

"Now I want you to uncross your arms like I did. Last night, Javier distracted me, so I won't look at you, and I won't see it coming." As he turned, she caught a profile where a tiny bump interrupted the line of his nose.

In her mind, she counted to three, then dropped her arms as fast as she could.

Chris's arms crossed, and he let go. "See?"

"You didn't just let me go?"

"Nope. Crossing or uncrossing arms when you can use it can give you an advantage. Um—" Chris stepped back. His mouth closed on whatever else he would have said.

"But?"

"I could have recaptured you." He put his hands in his pockets. "Teach me more?"

He shook his head. "That is what classes are for. You should learn from someone else."

"I've taken self-defense classes before."

"Were they taught by men? Or women?"

"Mostly men. A female police officer taught one." Most of the courses she'd taken had been focused on keeping a cockpit secure.

"Hastings utilizes our female bodyguards to teach the class since the students are mostly female. I guarantee it will be different from any other class you've had."

"It probably won't fit my schedule anyway. I know the ones that came with our apartment lease don't. At least not this month. I'm working every Saturday."

"You can talk to Javier about another time. The building classes are here on site, but Hastings conducts mid-week classes you could join. As far as the advanced classes, you should call ZoElle. They are by appointment only."

Tian stood and gathered her things. "You really want me to take this class, don't you?"

"I think every woman should be able to defend herself. I mean every person. I'm not trying to say that women are weaker. They are not." Chris's face reddened. "I'm getting myself in trouble here, aren't I?"

"A little. But it's fun watching you try to talk yourself out of it." Almost as fun as watching him swim. "If it makes you feel better, I'll call today."

"It does." He held open the door, and they left the gym together.

Dr. Linn tipped her head, waiting for Chris's answer to her question. The petite woman scared most of the employees at Hastings more than a sniper threat. The gray-haired psychologist missed nothing. She had the power to end careers. Never had that been a possibility for Chris. He'd never taken down anyone who hadn't posed a genuine threat before, either.

"Right before she came into the room, I was feeling frustrated."

"Why?"

Chris leaned forward in his chair. "I was on the phone with customer service, trying to figure out how my earbuds turned into an unidentifiable object."

"And she lunged at you, yelling?"

"She was trying to grab the object out of my hands. I misjudged her trajectory."

Dr. Linn looked up from her notepad. "So, what was the object?"

"A menstrual cup?" The words came out as a mumble.

"What?"

Not wanting to repeat himself again, Chris annunciated each word clearly. "A menstrual cup."

The corner of Dr. Linn's mouth twitched as she ducked her head behind her notepad. Still, the first notes of laughter escaped from her mouth. "I'm sorry. I shouldn't laugh. I assume she yelled pretty loudly."

"Yes, she did. It didn't register what she'd said for a moment."

"Was she injured?"

"No. I only used enough force to deflect her attack, or what I thought was an attack. I think I scared her more than anything. It scared me. I've never done anything like this before. Sometimes when I'm helping with the recipients of Mrs. Gooding's foundation, I want to find their abusers and attackers and give them more than a piece of my mind. And in one second, I became one of them. I didn't ever think…" Chris buried his head in his hands. He didn't want Dr. Linn to see how broken he felt. "I didn't think I could ever be one."

Several moments passed before Dr. Linn spoke. "Chris, will you look at me?"

Chris raised his head.

"From your report to Hastings and what you have said, as well as my interview with Javier, I wouldn't categorize what happened as abuse."

"Then why do I feel so bad?"

"Would you feel this way if she had been male?"

"Depends."

"On what?"

"Size, skill level. I mean, if it had been Javier or another body-guard, then they would have deserved it. They know not to yell and jump at a person. And if it had been one of the female guards, I would have defended myself too. Have you ever seen Abbie, Deirdre, or ZoElle take some guy down? I've been on the receiving end, and they are dangerous."

"You used the term 'defending yourself.' Explain that more."

"My first thought was that she was attacking me. I reacted badly."

Dr. Linn let him continue as he described his attempt at an apology and running into her that morning in the gym.

"I think she's forgiven me. She didn't seem afraid of me when I showed her the move to break my hold. She asked me to teach her more. I told her I can't."

"Why can't you?"

Because I am attracted to her. He certainly couldn't tell the doctor that. "I don't think I'd be objective. I'd either go too easy on her or too hard."

"Well, Chris, I believe you are thinking pretty clearly. I am going to recommend to Hastings that you are fit for full duty. I'll send my recommendations over to ZoElle this afternoon."

"Recommendations? Plural?"

"Yes. I took the advanced protection class years ago. I've seen Abbie in action and I know what the role of the assistants are in that class. Despite your saying you shouldn't be involved in the other Christian's training, I think that is exactly what you need, in a controlled environment."

"But…" How do you tell a therapist you are attracted to the one woman you can never date, without telling your therapist, and that the less time you spend together, the better for your sanity? Somewhere on TikTok, someone must have an answer to the question.

Dr. Linn raised her brow. "But?"

"It won't work because I am attracted to Tian." He allowed himself to say her name this time.

"And I am glad you are admitting it. However, before you ask, I have no advice on what you should do with that truth."

"I wasn't going to ask."

"It doesn't change my opinion that you should be an assistant for her class."

Arguing with Dr. Linn wouldn't work. His only chance was to convince ZoElle it was a bad idea to have him in the class—if he could do it without admitting his attraction to the client.

Five

A PILOT'S LIFE SHOULDN'T REVOLVE around food. Day three of a four-day was always the hardest for Tian. She'd spent two nights in hotels, and the last of her prepared meals were gone. Eating healthy on the road or in the sky was tricky. Occasionally, a hotel would be close enough to a grocery store to pick up fresh fruit or vegetables. The third night was the eat-out night, which usually meant depending on the location, either airport food, an expensive restaurant, or fast food. Delivery usually fell under the category of expensive. Today was different, though. She was flying back into O'Hare and switching crews and planes to go to Seattle. The odd schedule, created by the time off she took for the funeral, meant her roommates could bring her food and swap out her empty containers. This pathetic fact was the highlight of her work week. She needed a different focus than food and flying.

Perhaps she should start an online course or find a new podcast. The captain's voice through her headphones brought her thoughts back to the present. It was time for the pre-landing checks. Captain Rochester wasn't one for conversation, at least not with her. According to rumor, his wife had given him a second chance several years ago. Now he avoided any friendship with any female working for Legacy Air.

The landing and post-flight were as routine as they came. Tian gathered her things and followed Captain Rochester up the jetway. He paused halfway up.

"Thanks, Johnson, for not talking my ear off. And in my book, it doesn't matter who your old man is, you're one of the best FO's I work with." He touched his cap in salute and continued on, leaving Tian stunned for a moment. They'd flown together for two days and that was the longest sentence Rochester uttered.

Brit stood at the gate desk. "I thought you got lost coming off the plane."

"No. Just walked slowly. Did you bring my food?"

"Of course. I even traded gates, so I could tell you I put it in the pilots' lounge fridge. You can drop your dirty containers off with Simone."

"Thanks. You're the best."

Brit rolled her eyes. "Of course I am."

Tian walked a few gates down and swiped her badge to open an unmarked door leading to an unadorned hallway. A dozen other pilots made use of the lounge. Most of them were on the computers, checking the weather or flight plans. Brit failed to mention the huge note she'd left on the three food containers, cursing any pilot who touched them with a bumpier ride than a camel with fleas running from a hippo. As if such a scenario were possible. Tian took the containers over to a corner and repacked her bag. A first officer she didn't recognize came over. He didn't look old enough to be out of high school, let alone have enough flying hours to be an FO.

"You take your food seriously."

"Don't we all?"

He shrugged. "It's easier to buy food wherever I am going."

"Where are you going?"

"South Bend."

As she'd suspected, he was new. Only the newest of pilots would have a thirty minute flight to an airport so close the average commuter could drive faster than the time it would take to park, go through security, and fly.

Tian zipped up her suitcase. "Have a pleasant flight."

She stored her bags in one of the pilot lockers and headed to the scheduling office. Simone frowned as she talked into her headset. She pointed to the corner of her desk. Tian placed her empty food containers in the empty spot. Simone ended the call.

"What is wrong?" asked Tian.

"PR and the attorneys are having a tug-o-war, and I'm the rope. Oh, and this resurfaced today." Simone held up her cell phone open to a video that duetted last fall's airplane assault with an old Brady Bunch clip of Marsha yelling, "My nose!" on repeat.

"That stinks."

Simone tucked her phone away. "PR likes it. They say it garners sympathy. I want to return to the flight crew. This job is fine, but—"

"You belong in the sky."

"Exactly." Simone let out a sigh. "I was supposed to be back upstairs by now."

"I know."

"Maybe I'll learn something in our defense class tomorrow. Too bad you won't be there."

"I'll take mine on Tuesday. I've got to run. I still haven't made it to the restroom, and I need to check the computer before I meet the captain for my next flight. See ya." Tian hurried down the hall. Nothing like the mention of a restroom to remind one how badly they needed one. Passengers weren't the only ones who avoided airplane lavatories.

Back in the pilot's lounge, she claimed a computer and completed the necessary checks for the flight to Seattle. The storm over Montana might stir up some turbulence, but nothing to worry about, and better than that, there was no expected precipitation this evening at Sea-Tac. Unbelievable for Seattle to have a clear night in January. Tian checked the local Seattle news website to verify the forecast.

"You know that isn't the official weather." A deep voice rumbled like thunder behind her.

"Yes, but any time I see a forecast for good weather in January, I want a second opinion." Tian switched her tabs back and then turned to see who spoke.

She'd only seen a photo of the dark and dimpled Captain Cook before. The poor man, his name conjured cartoon images of sugar-coated cereal and one-handed pirates, without his name belonging to either. Simone giggled every time she said his name and recited his stats. Former Air Force, mid-thirties, six-one, and very single. "Nice to meet you. I'm Tian Johnson, your FO."

His brow furrowed for a split second. "I guess I should have looked you up in the company directory. I expected Christian Johnson to look different."

"You and everyone else." With less than seven percent of commercial pilots being female, everyone expected a male First Officer.

He inclined his head to the table on the far wall. "Let's go find our plane."

Too bad he was a pilot. Tian vowed never to date another pilot, and this one was the first one to tempt her since... The He-She-Never-Named, AKA The Cheater.

While Chris applauded the Ogilvies' decision not to use the company jet for trips involving a single person, flying commercial presented an entire other set of problems. For Mrs. Ogilvie's three-day trip to Seattle, she needed four bodyguards to rotate in twelve-hour shifts. This meant sending two ahead or subcontracting with a local firm. Colin Oglivie's business contact in Seattle, Tate Gilman, had similar security needs, so they contracted with his firm. Since the other firm couldn't provide a female bodyguard, Dana would be the second for this trip. She met him in the security room of Two Garden Tower.

"I can't believe how excited I am about this assignment. The kids are great, but not having to read picture books for the entire weekend and getting paid for that blessed break is the best."

"You miss regular service?" Chris handed her one of the airline-approved gun safes.

"Yes and no. I like the kids, but there is a reason I didn't go to college to become an elementary ed teacher." Dana broke down her weapon. "I always worry the airline will lose my checked luggage when I fly for work."

"Same. I vote for the less environmentally friendly private plane option so I can carry."

"At least you get to ride first class."

"Only because I look more formidable in a suit than you do." In public situations, appearing the part of a personal protector was as valuable as the weapon he locked in the case.

"Which is why I can fly in my comfy jeans."

"See, coach has its perks."

"Tell me that when I'm served pretzels for dinner." Dana closed and locked her case. "I'll see you onboard. Don't be surprised when I pretend not to know you."

Chris laughed and followed her from the room. Melanie Hastings, Alan's mother and security strategist, had designed the "hidden security plan" years ago. A second bodyguard in plain sight that blended in had proven to be the key factor in a protection detail more than once.

Most of the occupants in the airport VIP lounge kept to themselves. Two other people had personal protection traveling with them. Chris recognized the bodyguards, but not their principals.

Mrs. Ogilvie sighed. "Are you going to look that glum the entire trip?"

"No, ma'am."

"You can call me Candace. You've been with me a year, and I still don't like being called ma'am."

"Trying to keep it professional."

"Calling me by my name is still professional. It isn't like you can succumb to the Hastings curse. One, I am happily married; and two, you are not a Hastings."

Chris laughed. All five Hastings children had married their clients, which had then become a running joke among the personal security community. "You forgot to mention number three. Your husband will find a creative way to guarantee I never work again."

"That was a given. Colin is very protective." Candace sipped from her glass of water.

Their flight was announced. Chris finished his water and stood. "May I escort you to the plane?"

Candace grabbed the handle of her computer bag. "You'd better."

As planned, they arrived when the final passengers lined up. By boarding near the last, very few people would see Candace was on board. Dana wasn't in the waiting area. Chris assumed she was already on the plane as planned.

They scanned their boarding passes and entered the jetway. A flight attendant greeted them. Candace stopped in the aisle in front of 3A and 3B. A large woman sat feeding a fluffy white lap dog a kibble treat.

Chris tapped Candace's shoulder and nodded for her to move back another step. "Excuse me. You are in our seats."

"No, I am in my seats. Aren't we Thor?"

The dog yapped at him.

"Is there a problem?" asked the flight attendant. "Oh. You need to put your dog back in your carrier."

The woman gathered the dog to her chest. "Thor doesn't like being in a cage."

"FAA regulations require that pets ride in approved carriers under the seat in front of you." The attendant turned to Chris. "May I help you find your seat?"

Chris swiped his phone to his seat assignment. "We have found our seats."

The attendant held out her hand to the dog's mom. "May I see your boarding pass?"

The woman huffed. The dog copied her. "These seats were open."

"Your boarding pass, please."

"The man on TickityTacky said this is how to get a free upgrade. You wait until everyone is on and move." The dog yapped his agreement.

TikTok? Chris fought to keep his bodyguard face in place.

"I need you to show me your boarding pass." The attendant's voice was tight, her smile unnaturally wide.

A male flight attendant joined them from coach and stood behind Chris.

"This is persecution. You are all canine-phobic!"

"Ms. —" started the female attendant.

"I know my rights!"

"We cannot take off until you are in your seat and your dog is stowed properly. If you refuse, I'll need to inform the captain."

"The captain. I saw him. Yummy. I'd love to meet him." Dog mama looked Chris up and down. "He's not too bad either."

The attendant from coach nodded to the other one. She picked up the phone to the cockpit. A moment later, the door opened and out stepped… Tian?

Her gaze locked with his, and Chris realized he'd spoken out loud. Under her cap, her brow furrowed. "I am First Officer Johnson. The captain has asked me to remove you and your dog from the plane."

"He can't do that. I paid to be on this plane."

"Mrs. Crandall, the captain has asked that you leave this plane." Tian spoke with a firmness that caused Chris to freeze.

"How do you know my name?"

Tian smiled. "Do you need assistance with your bags?"

The pounding of feet on the jetway announced the arrival of police officers.

Tian two finger pointed behind Candace. "Chaz, please close the curtain for a moment. Mrs. Ogilvie and Mr. Johnson, if you wouldn't mind moving back a bit?"

"Fine! I'll go back to my seat." The woman stood and clutched her dog.

"That is no longer an option. The captain has asked that you leave his ship." Tian let the security officers by.

The officers walked the wailing woman and her yapping dog from the plane. The first flight attendant gathered the woman's pet carrier and purse while Chaz checked the overhead bin. Tian produced a container of cleansing wipes, and Chaz gave the seats a quick cleaning.

"On behalf of Legacy Air, our sincerest apologies." She addressed the first-class cabin before returning to the cockpit.

Candace sat in the window seat as Chris put her bag in the overhead bin. The captain made the standard announcement to the flight crew to prepare the plane for departure.

"That was a novel experience," said Candace as Chris buckled his seat belt.

"Yes, it was." His phone vibrated. The Hastings security app. Chris checked it quickly since they were still on the ground.

Dana: What happened? And good call on getting them to close the curtain. I don't think anyone recognized MsO.

Chris: Funny story about a woman and a dog. I'll explain later.

The flight attendant reminded everyone to put their devices in airplane mode. Chris switched over to the airplane Wi-Fi.

Candace offered Chris a stick of gum. "I can't do take-offs without some."

"Thanks."

"So how do you know the pilot?"

"What makes you think I know her?" This was the problem with being on first names with the principal.

"You said her name, and your observing-everything face cracked for a moment. She seemed surprised to see you, too."

"She moved into the building last weekend."

"Anything to do with your late-night need for a stuffed bear?" Candace smiled like the proverbial spider to the fly. She knew he was trapped, and she would eventually pull the story out of him. Maybe he should have opted to have Dana fly first class.

Six

Captain Cook completed his announcements to the passengers. Now that they had reached cruising altitude, the plane followed its programmed path westward. Tian checked the instrument panel as the captain turned many of the plane's functions over to autopilot.

The captain flipped the last switch and relaxed in his seat. "And here I thought we were going to have an uneventful flight. It started out with having to kick a dog off. Not what I was expecting today. I hope it is our quota for odd."

"Why did you send me back instead of having the cabin steward take care of things? She had things under control."

"Are you questioning my methods?"

"No. I'm trying to understand. Most pilots I've worked with trust their crew enough to let them handle the situation."

"It isn't a matter of trust. I was more concerned about the ticket holder to seat 3B. He checked a gun in his luggage through to Seattle. And since he is flying with a person of note, I assumed he was personal security. I don't trust bodyguards to act rationally. I assumed that a show of authority would keep him in his place."

Tian stared out of the window at the blanket of clouds. From here, they looked as warm and inviting as a down comforter, yet she knew viewed from below they were ominous in their threat to bring another winter storm to the upper Midwest. "I see your reasoning. However, this bodyguard looked more amused than anything."

"Still, I've seen too many paid thugs go overboard when it wasn't necessary."

"Then why didn't you go?"

"One, to leave a back-up plan; and two, you've got a prettier face."

Unsure of where to catalog that piece of conversation, Tian let it drop. "So, how did you earn your pilot's license?"

Captain Cook laughed. "You're either terrible at changing the subject or super curious."

"Probably terrible at changing the subject. I've already heard that you are a former Air Force pilot."

"What else have you heard?"

"I believe most of what I've heard is classified." Tian teased.

"Yes, I'm single."

At least he was direct. "No. I don't date within the airline, and the only trait of my father's I inherited is my love of flying."

"You're one of those Johnsons?"

"You mean the ones that put nepotism in Legacy Air? Yes, I am. Which means now you will be judging me the rest of the flight to decide if I got my job because I was a female, because I'm a Johnson, or both."

"What if you got your job because you're good?"

"No one ever assumes that when they first meet me."

"Kind of like when pilots hear I flew for Uncle Sam—they assume I'm cocky?"

"Is that a rhetorical question?"

"Well, First Officer Johnson, if you promise not to judge me by my stereotype, I won't judge you by yours."

"Sounds like a deal."

"Now, what did you mean that the only thing you got from your father was his love of flying?"

"Have you ever met my father?"

The captain shook his head no.

"My father is the cliché pilot of all the cliché pilots. My mother was a flight attendant, his second wife was a passenger, his third wife was a desk agent, and his fourth wife was another flight attendant. I think you see the pattern … Well, you get the idea. I have six half-siblings that I know of."

The captain whistled in a low tone. "Now I know why someone tried to bet me I couldn't get you to go out to dinner with me."

"Somebody is betting on me?" She ran through the faces of the pilots in the lounge, wondering who knew enough about her to put the captain up to such a bet.

"More like they were betting against me."

Tian didn't want to know. "So, what is the favorite place you've ever been?"

"Changing the subject again?" He laughed, and the conversation moved on to planes and landing strips.

Somewhere over the Rockies, an alert from the Denver Air Traffic control tower sounded. Through her headphones, Tian listened as the captain conversed. Dread grew in the pit of her stomach. When the conversation ended, they looked at each other in silence.

"Put the new coordinates in," Captain Cook said. "I'll alert the crew and try to give them a heads up."

With Wi-Fi, some passengers might already be hearing rumors and asking questions.

Tian listened as he explained the situation over the crew's phone. Then he switched to the PA system for the general announcement.

The Hastings's app pinged a three-tone beep. Something was wrong. Chris swiped to read the screen.

Above him, the speakers crackled.

"This is your captain, Joshua Cook. I have an important announcement. We have just received word that the Seattle-Tacoma airport is closing to all incoming planes because of a bomb threat at the airport. Our plane is being diverted to Spokane, Washington. Nothing is wrong with our plane, and we are not in any danger. I will update you as I know more. I repeat, nothing is wrong with our plane, and we are not in any danger—we are only being diverted."

His words mirrored those on Chris's phone screen. He shared the screen with Candace. Like the captain, he believed that sharing the truth was better than sugar-coating things. "With your permission, I'll ask Hastings to book a hotel and a car in Spokane."

"Probably wise."

He tapped the message into his phone.

Most of the passengers began to talk to those around them. Speculations ran rampant.

The seat belt sign flashed.

The flight attendant picked up the phone. "Please remain seated with your seat belt fastened. We will pass through the cabin to collect all of your empty containers. For those of you worried about missing connections, we would like to point out that the plane for your connecting flight is also being diverted. The captain has promised to give us news as soon as he hears. And remember, not everything you read on social media is true. I know this because I saw a quote from President Lincoln saying so."

A smattering of laughter dispersed some of the tension.

Chris's phone pinged again.

> Hastings: Wow, availability is going fast. I found two side by side Jr. suites with a king and a couch in each. Or a corner suite with two kings and a couch. Ask MsO.

Chris showed the phone to Candace.

"You need a better code name for me. I feel like some sort of off brand cereal. MsO meal. Either way, one of you ends up on a couch. My apologies."

> Hastings: Found this—a 2-bedroom king suite with an adjoin-
> ing standard double queen room.

Candace pointed at the screen. "That one."

> Chris: Book it.

> Hastings: Done. Also rented an SUV.

"I wonder what everyone else does for a hotel?" asked Candace. "Hopefully, the airlines can put them up."

"Hard to believe that four years ago, I would have planned to curl up in a corner of an airport and sit it out. Of course, I would have also been with my roommates. Now, I am probably booking the best room left in the city."

His phone vibrated.

> Dana: Do the kids know?

> Hastings: Negative. MrO wants to wait until we have
> more information.

Candace read the screen. "Ask Hastings to tell M-R-O that M-S-O agrees."

Chris typed the message into his phone. He should have known when he met Thor that his day would be weird.

Tian rubbed her temples after sitting on the tarmac for an hour before they could deplane. Most of the passengers had been polite about everything. That was two hours ago. For the last hour, she'd sat in an overcrowded conference room with other pilots waiting for news. Finally, an airport official entered.

"Preliminary sweeps of the Seattle-Tacoma Airport have found nothing. TSA and Homeland are conducting a full sweep, and the plan is to accept flights at 07:00 tomorrow morning. We are in contact with your companies to work on schedules for your departures. I suggest you all go find your eight hours of sleep so you can be patient with us. We haven't had this many planes on the ground at this airport in twenty years. Our goal is to see you on your way efficiently and safely."

Somewhere someone deserved a very long jail term for shutting down the airport and messing up flights for the next two to three days.

"We knew that an hour ago." A pilot from a competing airline on her right shut his iPad. He turned to her. "If they run out of hotel rooms, you can share mine."

Tian narrowed her eyes. "You've had an hour and a half to come up with a pickup line, and that was the best you've got?"

"It was worth a try."

She stood and walked away, keenly aware that she was the only female in the room. With females composing less than ten percent of all commercial pilots, it happened often enough. She joined Captain Cook. She should call him Joshua, but the other name was more fun. He stood with the ten other Legacy Air pilots.

One held up his phone. "Bless the people in scheduling, they found rooms for us in a five-star. I guess the passengers filled up most of the rooms in town."

A bounce returned to Tian's step. She'd been dreading getting the dregs of whatever Spokane offered. The cabin crew had left an hour ago and booked the last three rooms at one of the standard hotels. Although the union and the airlines had an agreement about what were acceptable accommodations, the availability clause often meant that a lesser room could be chosen in emergency situations.

The hotel was larger than she expected. She stood in line with the others for her room keys. The pasted-on smiles of the front desk staff told her this had not been an easy evening for them either.

"Name?"

"Christian Johnson."

"I don't have a room for you."

"What?"

The man behind the counter tapped his keyboard. As the last pilots got their keys, the lines on either side of her shrunk. The man behind the counter went into the back room.

Captain Cook stopped. "Problem?"

"I'm sure they'll figure it out in a minute."

"Some of us are going out for dinner. Do you want to join us?" He put his hands up. "Not a pickup line. Only a group of hungry aviators."

"No, thanks. I have a headache, and I packed my dinner."

"See you in the morning then."

The desk agent returned with an older woman. She took over his keyboard. "There it is. Christian Johnson, just like I told you."

"But—"

The woman cut him off with a glare. "Sorry about the wait, Captain."

"I'm a First Officer. Still earning my stripes."

"But you're a pilot, though, right?"

"Yes." Tian took the offered key.

"Have a good evening."

The elevator doors closed, and she stretched her arms, not caring that security probably monitored her. The hallway carpet was unexpectedly plush and devoid of the petri dish-style patterns found in so many hotels. Tian tapped the key card on the lock and opened the door.

A country song played. Someone must have set the radio alarm wrong. She pulled her suitcase into the room and set it on the luggage stand. As unlikely as a room in a five-star was to have bedbugs, she always checked first. Tian yanked off the covers on the bottom corner. No signs of the obnoxious little creatures. Once bitten, twice or twenty times cautious. While tucking the sheets back in, she heard a noise behind her and realized the music had stopped. She whirled around and screamed at the towel-clad man exiting the bathroom area.

"What are you doing in my room?" Their questions mingled.

From his wet hair and bare torso, it was very obvious what Chris had been doing. Fortunately for both of them, the hotel also provided larger than standard towels. Someone pounded on the door connecting to an adjoining room.

Chris knocked back twice.

"What—" Tian needed answers. Many women probably had a fantasy of having a hot guy walk out of their shower, but not her. At least not until now.

"Hold that thought." Chris stepped back into the bathroom and slammed the door. Tian bit her lip, not sure if she should laugh or not. Obviously, there had been a mix-up at the registration desk. She crossed the room and sat in the chair next to the windows, closed her eyes, and kneaded her temples.

Chris emerged a moment later clad in a pair of black sweats and a gray t-shirt, typing on his phone. "Obviously, they gave you a key to my room."

"Or they gave you a key to mine."

He shook his head and pointed to the door. "Mrs. Ogilvie's suite. It was Dana pounding on the door."

"Dana, as in lives-in-our-building and was on our plane?" The woman hadn't indicated she knew Chris in the gym. Was she crushing on him, too?

"Dana, as in the other half of the security team."

"She didn't tell me she knew you." Tian waved her hand. "Doesn't matter. I guess I better go figure my room situation out."

"Let me put on my shoes, and I'll go with you. They probably won't believe you if I am not there with my ID."

Chris sat on the end of the bugless bed. Tian rubbed her temples again.

"Headache?"

"Growing by the minute. I just need to eat and sleep."

"You haven't eaten yet?" He stood.

Tian retrieved her bags from the stand. "I had a snack on the plane. Yes, it was the cookies. I have my dinner in here. Microwavable."

He held open the door. "You travel with your own food?"

"When I can. Normally by the third day of a four-day flight schedule, I am left with whatever I can buy, but I had a plane change at O'Hare, and Brit brought me replacements."

"I didn't realize you were a pilot."

"I thought I told you I flew."

"I assumed you were on a flight crew." The elevator door swished open. "Sorry, I shouldn't have."

"You and everyone else." Tian rubbed the back of her neck—anything to release the tension.

The man who'd helped her earlier stood behind the desk. "May I help you?"

"We have a slight problem. We have the same name and somehow Miss Johnson was given a key to my room."

"Let me get the manager."

The manager hustled out of the back office. The man trailed behind, talking quickly. "…what I tried to explain."

The woman glared at him. "What is the problem?"

Seven

"I am Christian Johnson, and this is First Officer Christian Johnson. Through some mix up, someone accidentally put her in my room."

"But…but…" The manager typed on the keyboard. "When the airline sent over their list, your name was already in the system…"

Tian leaned on the desk, her face drained of color. "You don't have any more rooms?"

"No. There was a bomb threat…Oh you probably know." The manager's brisk demeanor dropped with every answer.

Tian sighed. "What am I supposed to do?"

"What you pilot types always end up doing," muttered the woman.

Tian's jaw dropped.

"I mean, there are two beds in the room. Can you work it out? I can remove the charges."

Chris read the woman's name tag. "Darleen, after you apologize to Miss Johnson, your assistant is going to help us find a solution. And I will write a very nice letter, commending, um"—he read the man's name tag— "Paulo for his help."

Darleen lifted her chin. "Like anyone will care about your letter."

Sweats were not nearly as intimidating as his suit, but Chris folded his arms and gave her the glare. The woman slunk back into her office without apology.

"I am so sorry, miss. My boss —" Paulo looked over his shoulder.

Tian leaned more into the counter.

Chris touched her elbow. "Why don't you sit down? Paulo and I will figure something out."

Tian nodded and walked over to the nearest of the lobby chairs. Whatever snack she'd had earlier wasn't enough. "Paulo, do you have a candy bar or anything back there?"

"Warm chocolate chip cookies?"

"May I have one?"

"Sure." He went into the back office and returned with a plate of chocolate goodness and a two pint bottles of milk. Chris took them over to Tian. "Eat."

"Neanderthal much?" Her soft smile took the bite out of what could have been an insult. She took a bite of the cookie, and her smile grew.

Chris returned to the counter. "Any options for us, Paulo?"

"Every room is full. I don't even have a foldaway bed left."

Chris rubbed his face. There was an option, if Candace would agree. However, his name double was another matter.

"Come on. You have a room." Chris extended his hand.

Being rescued wasn't her style. If it wasn't for her headache, she'd tell him so. Instead, she took his hand and stood. She couldn't remember the last time someone offered their assistance. Maybe it was a bodyguard thing. She dropped his hand and grabbed her suitcase.

"You have chocolate—" He pointed to the side of his own mouth.

The cookie and milk hadn't diminished her headache, but at least it wasn't growing. Tian pulled the tissue she'd used to wipe her fingers from her pocket and wiped her mouth. "Did I get it?"

Chris shook his head and guided her hand to the right place. "There."

He removed his hand from hers, but the connection remained. Her pounding head must be playing with her hormones, as they were sending all sorts of signals to her mind and heart.

They entered the elevator. Tian stared at the button Chris pushed for a moment before she realized it was the same floor they'd come from. "Where is my room?"

"We played musical chairs, or beds. You have the room I was in."

"Where are you going?"

"Mrs. Ogilvie and Dana have a two-bedroom suite, with a couch in a separate seating area. As far as security, taking the couch is a better option."

Tian closed her eyes against the fluorescent lights of the elevator. "So I am kicking you out of your bed? That isn't right."

"Actually, it is very selfish."

She opened one eye. "How?"

"If you don't sleep, you can't fly. And if you can't fly, we can't fly. Which means I should have driven to Seattle the moment we picked up the SUV. I don't like unplanned detours when working, so I need you to sleep."

His explanation was too logical. Not the friendly gesture she'd assumed. "Oh."

The elevator doors opened. Chris took her bag before she could. Per airline protocol, she never let anyone take her pilot bag. At least it was still in sight. He opened the door, set the bag inside, and handed her the key card.

"I'll clean out my stuff." He turned to the bathroom.

Tian set her suitcase back on the rack and unzipped it. The container holding her dinner sat on top. Asparagus chicken pasta didn't sound as appetizing as it had earlier. Her headache wanted a greasy hamburger and a chocolate shake—neither of which was remotely healthy comfort food. Which meant her headache wasn't merely a headache—it was PMS. Joy.

Not joy.

At least she knew why she felt so attracted to Chris. He'd rescued her and Mother Nature had an extra boost.

Chris exited the bathroom, his suit coat hanging from one arm and a plastic chain store bag in his hand. "I'll be back. Then I'll get out of your hair."

He knocked on the door to the adjoining suite. Dana opened it.

As soon as he exited, someone tapped on the open door. Mrs. Ogilvie. The woman she was inconveniencing stood in yoga pants and a t-shirt with a scarf tied around her head.

"Hi, I'm Candace. Chris said you have a headache. Do you need anything? I have some peppermint oil."

Dumbfounded. Tian stood frozen, holding her dinner container. "Mrs. Oglivie, I—"

The woman held up a hand. "One, it's Candace. Two, if the next words out of your mouth are to apologize for a situation that isn't your fault, stop. Three, it is my honor to meet you officially, not the other way around."

"Oh." Seriously, her vocabulary had shrunk to monosyllables in the last hour. At this rate, she'd have Mrs. Ogilvie complaining to the airline and end up having to take a drug and alcohol test before flying in the morning. Tian held up her container. "Dinner."

"It hurts to talk?" Mrs. Ogilvie didn't wait for an answer. "That is a severe headache. Dr. Pepper? Or a chocolate shake? Or my personal favorite—a Dr. Pepper, chocolate, and ice cream float."

"A what?" The combination sounded weirdly soothing.

"The perfect blend of caffeine for the headache and calcium to keep your stomach from getting upset. I try to avoid painkillers of any sort."

"I've never heard of that."

"Why don't you heat up your dinner, change, and come on over? By then, I'll have one for you." Candace waved and returned to the suite.

At some point during their conversation, Chris must have come back into the room. He exited the bathroom and tossed a cleaning wipe in the trash. "Not as good as if housekeeping had come, but hopefully it is adequate."

"You cleaned the bathroom?" A guy who cleans up after himself. That was hotter than a dripping wet shirtless Chris.

He smiled. "Shut the adjoining door after me. I heard Candace tell you to come over when you are ready. No need to knock. The sitting area is on the other side. You won't walk in on anyone coming out of the shower."

Was she imagining it, or had he blushed?

Fifteen minutes later, Tian stepped tentatively into the suite. Her long hair was down and she wore a t-shirt and yoga pants, as she had when Chris first met her.

Candace looked up from her iPad. "Make yourself comfortable. I'll go make the floats."

Dana made space on the couch. "Hi. We met in the gym."

"I didn't realize you worked in personal security, too."

"Officially, I am one of the Ogilvie's nannies—or I have been for the last six months. But I've worked for Hastings for two years."

"No offense, but you don't look like a bodyguard." Tian sat at the end of the couch.

"That is the point. I blend in, go unnoticed. Which reminds me, thanks for closing the curtain to first class during the incident. I was trying to figure out how to block people's view of Candace."

"I didn't think of that. I didn't want a viral video from someone who could only see half of what was happening. No one in first class seemed to be filming, and they all looked pretty disgusted with Thor and his owner."

"Does that sort of thing happen often?" asked Candace as she handed Tian and Dana the first floats.

"When I started flying, not so much, but we are seeing it more and more. In December, we had three flights where we expelled passengers. The cabin crew isn't as likely to let things slide either. Last September, my cousin Simone, a flight attendant, was punched by a noncompliant passenger. Not only did they have to make an emergency landing, but he broke her nose and cheekbone."

Candace returned with her own float. "She's your roommate too, right?"

Tian's brows raised in surprise, Tian looked up. "How did you know?"

"Zoe Gooding is my cousin. Your cousin applied for one of her grants. I reviewed the application, as I always do for our building."

"Oh, I wondered how we got the apartment. I mean, I knew about the grant, but not the process." Once they realized Simone's stalker had located the building where they rented a crash pad with other pilots and flight attendants, they'd searched for a place with more security. The grant offered by Mrs. Gooding's foundation made it possible for them to move into a place that would have cost almost as much as their combined monthly salaries at a rate they could afford. "The ongoing local media and social media attention to your cousin was a factor. The rest is confidential. Not even these two know about it. I didn't tell Chris your name, which I understand now may have been a mistake."

Chris answered quickly. "Not your mistake."

Dana looked from one person to another. "Why do I feel I missed out on something?"

"Tonight isn't the first night someone confused me and Chris since we have the same names." Tian finished her drink and set the glass on a coaster.

"Oh, you're the woman Chris got the bear for! I hadn't made the connection," said Dana.

"You know about that?" asked Tian.

Candace tapped Tian's knee. "In the world I married into, they tell jokes about the maid and or the butler knowing too much. But let me tell you about the bodyguards..."

Until now, Chris had been content to observe the conversation. Before he could defend himself, Dana jumped in.

"Chris told me." Dana grinned. "He had to, or I wouldn't give him a bear."

"Any information I pass on is on a need-to-know basis." Chris tried to glower, but Candace's smile was too big.

"What I was going to say is that the bodyguards are really close, so they don't have many secrets."

"Thank you for the float. I feel bad about Chris sleeping on the couch"—she looked at her hands— "when there is a second bed in my room."

After what the manager had said about pilots, Chris wasn't going to suggest such a thing. He looked at Dana, hoping she'd bail him out.

"What if I take the extra queen?" Dana took his hint. "That gives Chris the second king over here and with the adjoining door, we'd be back to the same security scenario, and everyone gets an actual bed."

Dana's question was aimed as much at him as it was at Tian.

Tian's phone buzzed.

While she checked her screen, Chris nodded at Dana. "That works for me."

"It looks like I have a 6:00 a.m. shuttle to the airport so we can play musical gates. Your flight will be at 7:25." Tian stood. "Thanks, again for the float. I'm going to go to bed. Dana, don't worry about being too loud when you come in."

"I'll grab my stuff right now." Dana hurried into the other room.

Tian left the adjoining door open a few inches when she left the suite. After a moment, Chris realized he was staring at the door. He turned to find Candace studying him. She raised one painted eyebrow as she finished her float. "If you ever need another bear, she is definitely worth it."

Chris stood and took the empty glasses to the kitchenette. He didn't need a matchmaking principal when he was already trying to fight the pull of attraction. Tian wouldn't appreciate knowing how much more he wanted to do for her.

Eight

THE AFTERMATH OF THE CLOSING of Sea-Tac left Tian having to deadhead back to Chicago from Denver on a cargo plane late at o-dark-thirty Sunday morning as she'd run out of allotted flight hours. The first to board, she chose one of the window seats in the four-chair cabin. Chaz and two pilots from a competitor joined her. One pilot was the same one who'd offered to share his bed.

He stored his luggage and turned, obviously intent on sitting next to her.

Still holding his rolling bag, Chaz dove in front of him. "Thanks for saving this for me."

Tian stifled a laugh at the pilot's expression. "Anytime."

Chaz's intervention meant she could sleep on the flight without worrying about wandering hands.

They landed at O'Hare to falling snow. Tian opened her ride-share app, hoping to find someone with a four-wheel drive.

"My car is in employee parking if you want a ride." The offer came from the pilot she was trying to avoid. His gaze lingered on her chest area. She knew the type. No such thing as a free ride in his book.

"Thanks for the offer." Chaz answered before she could. "My roommate is already here. He's driving us."

She'd known Chaz for years—he'd been on several crews with Simone—but he'd never gone all protector on her before. What was with this weekend? She let Chris play the role. Now everyone was jumping on board.

Tian thanked the cargo pilots as she left the plane, then hurried to keep up with crossing the tarmac into the cargo company hangar. True to his word, Chaz's roommate Scott waited in his SUV. Tian climbed into the back seat.

"Scott, we're dropping Tian off. I had to listen to the most vile talk from one of those StuckUpAir pilots in the restroom in Denver. No way was he getting near my favorite female pilot. You should have seen me keep him from sitting next to her in the cargo. Girl, you stay far away from him."

Scott met her eyes in the rearview mirror. "Good thing she is my favorite, too. Even if we never get to fly together."

"Maybe when I reach captain, I can ask for you to be my FO." Tian teased. Since she'd graduated with Scott, they weren't likely to fly together soon as their flight hours would always be too close.

"Or I'll ask for you to be my FO." Scott smiled over his shoulder before turning back to the front. "I only brought one thermos of hot chocolate."

"Give it to our Tian. She needs it more. The things she has to put up with." Chaz handed back the thermos.

Tian put up her hand. "No, you keep it. I'm fine."

Chaz pulled it back. "If you're sure. I could use it to put me in a better mood. I still want to deck someone."

"I don't know that I want to know the rest of the story." Tian closed her eyes trying to block out the conversation. Chaz never ended until he made his point.

"This man would put your daddy to shame. I hear a lot when men think that women aren't around, but this guy was the worst. He insinuated you spent the night with some hulk of a man in Spokane. And I know you would never..."

Tian wondered if he had seen her with Chris entering the hotel room. "I didn't. But I had a funny room mix-up with a man who has my name. In fact, you met him. He was the man whose seat was stolen by Thor, the dog wonder."

Chaz turned in his seat. "Him?"

"What are the chances, right?"

"Oh, Scott, our girl finally has a crush on someone and he's got her name."

"Wait, how do you know I have a crush on him?"

"Besides, you admitting it? You should have seen your face when he said your name when you came out to deal with crazy dog-lady. I've never seen someone try so hard not to look at someone else in my life."

Tian leaned back against the headrest. "Chaz, it is way too early in the morning for this."

"It's never too early for love. Are you going to see him again?"

"He lives in my building."

Chaz snapped his fingers. "That's where I knew him from. He helped Simone and Brit move in. You had better see him again."

"What part of 'we have the same name' didn't you understand?"

"The part that means that should matter? A rose by any other name."

"Chaz..." She put as much warning as she could into her voice.

"Just saying a name isn't a good enough reason to not give the man a chance."

Chaz had a point.

ZoElle: 3 p.m. Don't be late.

Chris: I thought I had the day off.

ZoElle: You do. Helping with class doesn't count.

Chris switched his laundry. Apparently, his appeal to ignore Dr. Linn's advice had fallen upon deaf ears. He wasn't sure spending more time around Tian was a good idea. He'd spent way too much time thinking about her over the weekend, wondering if he'd overstepped arranging her room. Independent women didn't like men taking over for them—or at least that was what his sisters told him. Although he'd do it again in the same situation. That wasn't the reason he'd been avoiding Tian. The problem was he was attracted to her in a way he hadn't been attracted to a woman in a very long time. Earlier, when he noticed she was in the secure gym, he'd gone downstairs to the larger one.

The chances of getting through the self-defense class without talking to her were zero. The more he talked to her, the more he wanted to, and why was he fighting it?

If he was a gentleman, he'd offer her a ride over to Hastings, so she didn't have to take a taxi.

He may or may not have used Javier's login to see if she was in the common areas of the building before going to the store that morning. The computer told him she didn't have an assigned parking space or a car. He logged out and texted Javier to change his password to something harder to break than Que$o4D1nn3r.

He hadn't crossed the ethical line and looked at her personal information. He had two choices if he wanted to offer Tian a ride to the Tuesday afternoon class. Either he could knock on the door or ask the front desk to call her. He should have stayed logged in to Javier's account for another minute. If he used the security desk to call, every Hastings employee in the greater Chicago area would know before the Tuesday night news aired. Knock on her door won.

No answer. Not even a shuffling of feet behind the door. Of course, if she'd remembered to use her building app, she would have seen him on the video feed. If he rang the buzzer, her roommates would receive alerts on their phones... nope.

As he walked back down the hall, the elevator pinged. Chris slowed his steps. Mrs. Whipple from 40C stepped out with her cat carrier. In a movie, Tian would have stepped off the elevator. Chris said his hellos and returned to his laundry.

A few moments later, the doorbell buzzed. He checked his app. Tian stood back from the door, tapping an envelope in her hand.

Chris opened the door. "Hey."

She held out the mail. "I think it is only junk mail, but it clearly says 40H so—"

"Thanks. I haven't seen anything for you."

"I use a virtual mailbox. They send me photos of my junk mail and I tell them to shred it or open it. I only send packages to my physical address."

"I'll remember that next time I receive a package. I just stopped by your place. Would you like a ride to the class?"

"The defense class?"

"Yes. I got recruited to help." Suddenly, he wasn't so annoyed with Dr. Linn's interference.

"No, thanks. I thought I'd walk. It is only 3/4 mile. I walk further than that at many airports, including O'Hare."

He needed to justify driving. "Inside miles differ from outside miles, especially when it is below freezing."

"Fair point. What if I hitchhike back?"

"I think part of the point of the class is to not hitchhike, but I'll offer you a ride, anyway."

"I am careful to only hitchhike with people I trust." She waved as she turned away.

Chris arrived early at Hastings and stopped by ZoElle's office. He tapped on the open door and waited for her to look up from one of several computer screens on her desk. "Anything I need to know before your class?"

"My class?" ZoElle removed her glasses. "Oh. I'm not teaching today. Abbie and Melanie are."

"Melanie Hastings is teaching with her daughter?" Chris had only met Melanie once at last year's company picnic. Of course, he'd seen and met Abbie Hastings Harmon since she was friends with MsO. Abbie was legendary in the personal security industry. Undoubtedly, some stories about her had been exaggerated in the five years since she left the industry after her marriage to media mogul Preston Harmon.

"Yes. They wanted a girls' night out."

"So they are teaching a self-defense class?" Teaching anything seemed an odd choice for a night out activity.

"They both taught some of the first classes I took when I started here as a receptionist. Melanie claims teaching is at the top of her fun list. And if you've ever met Abbie's triplets, you know that a few hours of sparring with adults is relaxing."

"I knew back in the day they did—"

"Back in the day? Careful, Johnson, you are going to make me feel old. I'll have to ask Alan to take you down." Fighting her husband would be a fair fight. He'd sparred with Alan before.

"I thought you took care of your own fights?"

"I am on desk duty for the next six months, before I semi-retire or change job titles. 'Mom' has a nice ring to it."

News the entire office had been waiting for. The failed fertility treatments hadn't been a secret. "Congratulations!"

"Thank you. You should get to the gym. Melanie and Abbie are already downstairs."

Chris opted to run down the stairs to the private gym and training area. To his surprise, Abbie was sparring with a man in safety gear. Her next move landed him on the mat.

"You lose."

"You cheated." The man removed his red foam sparring helmet. Judging by his facial features, he was obviously a Hastings, possibly a cousin, but one Chris hadn't met.

Abbie captured the man in a headlock and tousled the man's hair. "Oh, baby brother, that California living has made you soft. Sure you can't stay for class?"

"No. My princess awaits." He nodded at Chris. "It looks like you have help."

Abbie turned. "Johnson, right?"

Chris nodded.

"This is my brother, Andrew. He is too chicken to stick around for class."

"Careful, sis, or I'll give your boys sugar-coated sugar-bomb cereal for breakfast." The threat against Abbie's triplets was probably idle, but he'd seen the three-year-olds in action when Candace had taken her own son, Peter, for a playdate. Sugar was the last thing those bundles of energy needed. Andrew extended his hand. "Nice to meet you. In case no one has told you, watch out for my sister."

"Ha ha." Abbie launched a roundhouse kick to Andrew's posterior that lacked any force.

"Pardon my kids. I thought now that they had children of their own, they would all grow up. Obviously, I was wrong." Smile lines crinkled at the corner of Melanie Hastings's eyes. "We met last summer."

"Yes, we did."

"ZoElle gave me strict instructions that there is one student in this class whom you are not to help or touch. I assume you know who I am talking about?"

The condition was news to Chris. "Since I only know one person, yes."

"Good. I'll try to not make it obvious. Alex will also assist this afternoon."

After Alan, Alex was the only other Hastings brother to work full time. Even so, his presence was unexpected.

"Have you ever helped with one of these classes before?" asked Abbie.

"Last spring."

"The class is pretty basic. We will demonstrate various scenarios and the students will practice on the sparring dummies. I'll ask you to do things like steal my purse, etc. Got it?"

"Okay."

"You should pad up," said Melanie. "Abbie doesn't go easy."

"Sure?" The question in his voice contradicted the answer. The rumors couldn't be true. Her brother must have let her win the sparring match he'd witnessed.

"In review, what is your goal?"

"Get away!" Tian answered Melanie Hastings's question in unison with the other students.

"Good. No purse, no cell phone, no computer is worth your life. We didn't teach you as many moves as some classes do because statistically, you aren't going to practice those techniques on a daily, weekly, or monthly basis. And if you have to stop and think about them, you are not running. At my age," Melanie touched her graying hair, "I am not as fast as I used to be. Keeping in mind the basics is what I need."

"Homework time." Half the class frowned at Abbie's announcement. "Two things, before the next session of this class: exercise at least sixty minutes. I don't care how or what as long as you stretch for part of it. Two, push-ups. I know they are old fashioned, however, they require little space and no equipment. Do one more each day than you think you can. One of your best defenses is going to be to stay in shape. Any questions?"

The middle-aged man who'd come with his wife blurted out the next question. "Weren't you in the tabloids a few years back? They said you could take down a man twice your size. Was that truth or fiction?"

Abbie crossed her arms. "Somewhat exaggerated. At the time, I was working full time as a bodyguard and so my goal was for others' safety—which differs from what we're teaching in this class. Also, I have years of training."

"So lies." The man turned triumphantly to his wife.

Alex Hastings stepped forward. A threatening sort of confidence oozed off of him. "Not a lie. My sister beat me two out of three sparring matches last week. And I heard through the family grapevine that she trounced my younger brother earlier today."

"She is your twin. Of course you're going to defend her."

Tian shared a sympathetic look with the woman in a Bull's shirt. This man didn't know when to leave it be.

Abbie rolled her eyes. "Johnson? Have I ever sparred with you?"

"No."

"Put back on a safety helmet, please."

Chris appraised Abbie for a long moment. She also put on headgear.

"Okay, Johnson, your goal is to get past me to my brother. And you have thirty seconds to do it. If you are going easy on me, I will make sure you work the very worst shifts for the next month."

For a moment, Tian thought Chris might protest. Instead, he nodded and took a step forward. The next moment, he was lying on his back on the mat.

At his smack on the mat, there was a collective gasp.

Chris sat up and pulled off his helmet. He was laughing.

"I think you went easy on me."

"No, ma'am, I did not." He'd thought about it, but he wanted to know the truth for himself. "I didn't see that coming."

"Any more questions?" Abbie stared hard at the man who'd questioned her abilities.

The man looked away.

"Alright then. Have a good evening and stay aware."

Class had run a few minutes late. Tian stood in line to refill her water bottle.

Two women, obviously friends, eyed Chris. "I can't believe she flipped him on his back. I thought he was strong."

"He let her," scoffed the man.

Annoyed with the man, Tian jumped into the conversation. "He looked genuinely surprised to me."

"Good actor."

Tian sat to retie her perfectly tied shoes. The walk over had been colder than she'd expected. A lift back would be great, but joining the students who were talking to the Hastings like a flock of die-hard fans wasn't worth it. Two of the women were particularly interested in Chris. Keeping his arms crossed, he smiled and talked with them. Oddly, his body language wasn't flirting or open. The shorter of the two women touched his biceps more than once as she spoke. Each time she did, his expression became more stone-like. Interesting. As a pilot, she'd had a nauseating amount of experience watching people react to flirtation. The ones who were closed off were in committed, monogamous relationships or were not interested in the gender of the flirt. After another minute, the women gave up and left.

Chris came over and sat next to her on the bench. "What did you think?"

"After I got over the fact that Abbie Harmon was teaching the class, which explains why they collected our cellphones as we came in, it was good. I've taken several classes before. Mostly work related, so nothing new." Not wanting to dis the class, Tian continued, "But it was a great reminder."

Melanie Hastings came to join them. "Chris, ZoElle asked me to have you come up. She said you weren't answering your phone."

Chris pulled his phone out of his pocket. The screen was blank. He tapped it and frowned. "I'll go up now." He turned to Tian. "Meet you in the lobby, in ten?"

"Sure."

Melanie took Chris's place. "What a beautiful name? What is its origin?"

"My name is Christian. As you may know, there are a lot of Christians and even more Johnsons in the world."

The older woman smiled a warm, motherly kind of smile. "Of course. That is how you know Johnson. You're the one with the same name."

Heat flooded her face. "Does everyone in the office know about our incident?"

"No. ZoElle included it in her weekly report. My husband and I are almost silent partners. She felt we should have a heads up."

"He didn't hurt me. Only surprised me, but that's all. I am not pressing charges, if that is what you're worried about."

"I'm more worried that you should press and were intimidated. That's the last thing I want."

Tian bit her lip. She thought this was over. His employer did have a reason to be concerned if it had been something more between reviews, tell all videos, and attorneys, it seemed like everyone erred on the side of caution. "I've had a week to think about it. I don't feel there's a need. Especially because I wasn't hurt." All her interactions with Chris flew through her mind. He was definitely trying to prove he wasn't normally so aggressive, yet his actions seemed natural at the same time. "He wasn't being mean. Just reacting."

"You've taken defense training before, haven't you?" Melanie stood, and Tian followed suit.

"How did you know?"

The elevator opened, and Melanie pushed the key for the Hastings's main office. "I've taught for over thirty-five years. Ew, make that forty. Oh, that makes me feel old." She laughed good-naturedly. "I know when I am teaching a novice and when someone is taking a refresher."

"I've taken several mandatory defense classes because of my job. I'm a pilot."

"That is almost as rare as female security personnel used to be. When I started, you could count all the female bodyguards in Chicago on one hand. Getting taken seriously was difficult. How is it for you being a minority in your field?"

"Most of the male pilots are good about it. There are those who make passes. A few assume I can't fly and I was hired to fill a quota or that my family got me the job."

The elevator opened. "You are signed up for our advanced class, right?"

"Yes, if I can coordinate with my crazy schedule."

"I'm sure we can. I'll see you next week." Melanie disappeared into the back offices.

Tian retrieved her phone from the main desk and waited for her ride.

Nine

ZoElle held out her hand for Chris's phone. "That is so odd. This is the second phone to run out of batteries…" She plugged his phone into a charger and made a face. She opened the drawer in the credenza behind her and pulled out a box for the latest C&O phone. "Lucky you. This one won't be on the market until Thursday."

Chris waited while she switched out the SIM card. "Is this what you called me up here for?"

"Yes, your phone showed it was off the Hastings's app, and I knew you were in the building. I figured I should check."

"I need to get going, then."

"What's the rush?"

"I promised Tian I would give her a ride home."

ZoElle smiled and waved him out of the room.

Tian stood on the far side of the lobby reading the award plaques.

"I hope I didn't keep you waiting too long."

"I've only been here for a moment."

Chris held open the lobby door and pondered his next words. If she said no to his request, he could count on their acquaintance staying exactly where it was. They entered the elevator, and he pushed the button for the parking level. No one else was in the elevator. Chris took a deep breath.

"Did she really flip you?" Tian's question caught him off guard.

"As much as I hate to admit it, yes. I wasn't expecting her to flip me. Even if I heard she could." And saw the evidence when she had the brother pinned.

"You outweigh her by a hundred pounds."

"Less than one hundred pounds. It's like I told you last week, size isn't the only factor."

"So I could learn to take you down?"

"Yes, under the right circumstances, you could."

"I might have to make that my new goal."

"Would that mean I'd always be on guard? Expect it when I least expect it with you?"

Tian shook her head. "No. I think I'd like to do it once to prove that I could."

"If you want to, I think that we would have to do such a thing in the Hastings's gym. I'd want you to be fully geared up so you're not injured."

"Are you insinuating that I wouldn't be able to take you down?"

"No." Although it might take her a while to learn. "I would prefer that we do such a thing in a safe environment. Besides, don't you want witnesses to your triumph?"

Tian laughed at his remark. The elevators opened.

"That's my SUV." He used his key fob to flash the lights and unlock the doors. Chris rebooted his courage to ask the question he'd planned on asking in the elevator. "Would you like to catch a bite to eat?"

"Are you asking me out to dinner?"

"Not a date or anything. It's just dinner." Why did he say that? It was a date. And he wanted it to lead to others.

Tian looked at him sideways for a long second. "Yeah, I'd like to go to dinner with you. It would give us a good chance to talk."

"Do you have any place in mind?"

She shrugged. "Not really. This part of Chicago's completely new to me. I used to live out by the airport. Is there a place you recommend around here?"

"We could go to my brother-in-law's."

"Family?"

"No, restaurant. Pizza. His family has owned it for years. He runs it now, mostly. And if there's not a seat, he'll let us sit in the back room. They serve the best Chicago deep dish in the city."

"Have you ever noticed that everyone claims to have the best Chicago deep dish?"

"Most of them lie." Chris opened the passenger door for her.

As he pulled out of the parking space, she tapped the fluffy pink dice his niece had given him. "Nice vehicle. Is it yours or the company's?"

"This one's mine, hence my niece's gift to her favorite uncle. She kept the sparkly ones for herself."

He backed out of the garage, passing rows of dark SUVs. Some were company cars, others not.

"Does everyone drive an SUV?"

"Most of us. I think we all have SUVs because we all keep an extra go bag and things on hand. We never know where we'll end up working, even if they assign us to a dedicated team."

"What do you mean?"

"I mean, I could be enjoying a nice, lovely night off, having dinner with a new friend, and in the middle of it, my phone will ping and say there's been an emergency somewhere, and I have to leave to trade out with a crew."

"Does that happen often?"

"Often enough that my last girlfriend dumped me over it." Oversimplification, but he wasn't willing to share everything yet. "I changed positions in November and now my schedule is more predictable. Not 9 to 5, but I won't get a call to hop on a plane to join some musicians' security group at the last moment."

He pulled into a parking space in a lot two buildings down from the restaurant. "What about your schedule?"

"My schedule is pretty laid out by the beginning of the month. In the winter, it gets bumped around a bit more because of the weather. The FAA rules, flying hours, and too long on a tarmac here or a delayed flight there can mess things up. For example, the Seattle thing gave me an entire extra day of flying, and if I hadn't taken time off at the beginning of the month for my aunt's funeral, I would have had to give up some of my flight time later. Which reminds me, thank you for making sure I had a bed to sleep in the other night."

"No problem."

"I'm still a little embarrassed that you had to have Mrs. Ogilvie move her situation around."

"Don't be. I didn't want you to have to awkwardly share a room with me." They entered the restaurant, ending the conversation. He wanted to tell her he wouldn't have taken advantage of the situation if they had shared rooms. Probably just as well he couldn't. She might not believe him anyway.

They only had a five-minute wait for the next table.

"Did you grow up around here?" she asked.

"Yes and no. Mom grew up here, so summers with grandparents were here. We moved a lot. Then I lived with my grandparents here for my last two years of high school because my dad had an overseas position. My older brother and sister were at college. As for the rest of the family tree, I am an uncle to three adorable niblings. And you?"

"I'm an only child on my mom's side. On Dad's, I have six siblings that I know of."

Chris wasn't sure what to say to that. "Brit seems cool."

"She is. We try not to blame the siblings for Dad's philandering… but it is always this game of when-is-another-going-to-show-up. How did you get into personal security? Military?"

"No. Not fond of being a nomad. In high school, I was a C

student and studying for another four years wasn't my thing. I wasn't scholarship worthy in sports, but I figured I had size and speed on my side, so I fulfilled my kindergarten dream of becoming a policeman."

"How did you end up here?"

"After eight years in the force…" Chris struggled with how to word the next part. "The political atmosphere changed—correction, the *atmosphere* changed. In six months I was shot at three times because of my uniform. The last time, they didn't miss. After I got out of the hospital, I decided I needed a safer job, and my brother Zane convinced me that private security was the way to go—better benefits, better hours, and frankly, a whole lot less chance of being shot."

She winced. "How badly were you hurt?"

"Nothing a few stitches didn't fix."

"So in other words, it was either life threatening or a graze, and you have no intention of telling me which one."

"Worse than a graze and not life threatening." The small scar was barely noticeable.

The waiter brought their pizza.

Tian stirred her root beer with her straw. "Funny, the only time I drink root beer is when I have pizza. Must be one of those childhood things. I'm surprised you didn't order a beer."

She was fishing. Chris let her steer the conversation in hopes she would feel like moving the friendship along.

"I don't drink. I've seen alcohol mess up way too many lives."

"Another thing we have in common. I don't drink either." She didn't elaborate on her reasons any more than he did.

If only he hadn't pinned her at their first meeting. Just his luck to meet someone he could have a relationship with and to blow it before he knew her name. This called for a long game. An endless game. Could he go all in?

Tian ran out of questions. Predictably, he'd played high school football and baseball. He enjoyed swimming, but didn't join the swim team, and he hated black licorice. The last was another thing they had in common.

"Did you find out about your jury duty?" she asked.

"I have to fill out a lot of online forms to find out my selection date. They do most of it online now with video calls. It will be the end of February before I know anything."

"They must give people plenty of time because of work schedules."

Chris set his pizza slice on his plate. "I feel like I've been monopolizing the conversation. What is your favorite thing about your job?"

"I fell in love with flying before I could walk. Grandpa used to take me up in his plane. I was eleven the first time he let me touch the controls. Mom didn't want me following the family business, so I went to Bradford College. After a semester, I knew I wanted a degree in aviation."

"How did your mom react?"

"She wasn't happy, but she knew it was coming. Because I had my license already, I was ahead of the game, so to speak. Since Grandpa has his own plane, I could accumulate most of my 1500 flight hours easily. He also made sure that I was on with Legacy's regional service as my first job. Had I realized how many people would ridicule me for that choice..." Her voice faded off and she sipped the last of her root beer.

"You would have done things differently?"

"Probably not. I'm a fourth-generation pilot. My great grandpa was flying before World War II and was one of Legacy's first pilots. I have a photo of me sitting on his lap in a cockpit with his hat on when I was four. He'd already retired, but everyone thought it would be cute to let his first great grand fly with him." She used air quotes on the fly. "My grandpa and dad are in photos from that shoot too. Of course, I was not in the cockpit for takeoff or landing. It was before 9-11, so Dad brought me back in when they were at cruising altitude. Anyway, my point is, the only way I could have done things differently was to run away and join the Air Force and hope they let me fly."

"Wow. Four generations, that's cool."

"So I keep hearing."

"What did I say wrong?"

"Nothing. There was a huge magazine article and cable TV show a couple of months ago for Legacy Air's centennial celebration. The entire Johnson clan is part of the fun. Almost all my cousins over the age of twenty-one are involved in the airline somehow, but yours truly is the only female pilot in the mix. In May, I was featured in a full-page article in an airline magazine." She circled her finger in the air.

"Let me guess, you don't like the attention."

"No. Simone and Brit are not thrilled, either. None of us like the spotlight. It was hard on Simone because of the whole assault and lawsuit mess—I assume Javier told you that her stalkers are why we have the apartment. Brit and I don't need some blogger to realize how our mothers found out about each other."

Chris raised a brow but didn't ask.

"I'll tell you in the car."

He asked for the check, and Salvo came out from the back. "You know you can't pay here, especially if you're on a date. Your sister would make me sleep on the couch." He turned to Tian. "I am Salvo Conti. I am so pleased that Chris brought you here. He usually only comes with his bodyguard buddies."

"Nice to meet you. I'm Tian, and Chris was right. This was the best Chicago deep dish I've ever had."

"I knew I liked you." Salvo looked at their empty plates. "What is this? No dessert? I will get you the deep-dish brownie with the ice cream on the side to go."

Tian shook her head at Chris, who answered. "No, we don't need—"

"Nonsense. The night is young. You may still want dessert." Salvo hurried into the kitchen.

Tian put her coat back on. Salvo hurried back and handed Chris one bag, and Tian another. "Here it is. Only one, so you'll have to share. Chris, you have the brownie, keep it warm. Tian, you have the ice cream with a special ice pack to keep it cold. When you put them together, you make perfection."

No hint of innuendo marred his delivery yet somehow Salvo seemed to be talking about more than brownies and ice cream. They thanked him and left.

New falling snow greeted them as they exited. Once again, Chris held the door for her. It must be bodyguard training. Men rarely did that—at least not men she knew. As he walked close, his free hand brushed hers once before he took her hand in his. The warmth of the contact melted her already frozen fingers. Tian didn't regret leaving her gloves in her gym bag on the floor of Chris's car.

The parking lot was nearly empty. The lights on Chris's SUV flashed in response to his remote. As they approached, the tailgate lifted.

"We can put the dessert back here." He let go of her hand to take the ice cream from her.

Tian stepped back as the tailgate closed. Her shoe slipped. Before gravity pulled her down, Chris's arms were around her, pulling her into his sturdy form. She looked up into his eyes. They were as warm and inviting as that brownie would be.

"Careful," the fog from his breath warmed her face.

He may have been talking about the ice. Her heart took the warning in another way. She turned her head before she looked at him too long and noticed… Rats. Too late. She'd more than noticed his lips. Who could blame a girl? She'd have to be dead not to notice them or how protected she felt in his arms. Her last relationship had been two years ago. Did she trust Chris enough to take that next step? Was it wise? Not ready to commit, she took a tentative step out of his arms. He loosened his grip but didn't let her go completely.

"Are you okay?" He searched her eyes. Did he see how much she welcomed his touch?

"I will be." The words came out in puffy clouds filling the space between them.

"Of course, you have the fastest reflexes."

"At least this time they came in handy." He opened the door and dropped her hand.

Tian turned to face him, laying her hand on the center of his chest. Through his parka, she could feel his muscles. "Chris, you are more than forgiven. I know you didn't mean to hurt me." She rose to her tiptoes, keeping her other hand on the door for balance, and brushed a kiss on his jawline, safely in his cheek area. At least, that is what she told herself as she settled into her seat. Kissing a guy on the jaw didn't have the same effect it had on a girl, did it?

Ten

CHRIS SAT IN THE SECURITY office of Crawford and Ogilvie. Colin had a private meeting, meaning Chris was in one of those many long hours of being near and alert but not needed. He was literally getting paid to stand around all day, hoping he had nothing to do. Hoping for anything different was literally asking for trouble. He didn't have to watch all the monitors since the building security guards did that. He only had to watch the one on Colin's office until he emerged to go to the restaurant with his new…client? Business partner? Chris had no idea, and it wasn't his business to know.

His mind kept wandering back to last night when he and Tian had returned to the apartment building. Tian had asked if he could save the desert for tonight. She'd allowed him to walk her to her door but kept her hands occupied. What was he supposed to make of that? She was the one who'd pressed her lips to his face in a tantalizing kiss, soft as a snowflake.

His phone vibrated. To his amazement, it wasn't the Hastings's app. It was the standard text messaging.

> Unknown: Hey name-buddy. Javier gave me your number.
> I hope it is ok.

Wise move. She didn't give out her information in case of a misdial.

> Chris: I'd ask if my roommate is behaving himself..but that is pointless. I'm glad he gave you my number.

> Tian: I wanted to invite you to our apartment-warming Friday night, but I'll be en route to Hawaii.

> Chris: So you invited me to a party where you won't be, and then tell me you'll be some place better?

> Tian: Kinda. The rest of the message was that I wondered if you still wanted to do dessert tonight? I could make dinner. Today is my cooking day.

> Chris: Dinner sounds great. If everything goes to schedule, I should be off by seven. Is that too late?

> Tian: No, see you then.

> Chris: I'll text if I'll be later.

He put his phone back in his pocket and hoped that work didn't turn any more exciting than it was at the moment.

He got his wish. At 1855, Colin Ogilvie was safely back in the residence officially ending Chris's work day. Chris stopped at his apartment long enough to switch his suit for jeans and grab the dessert.

Brit answered the door. She buttoned her coat and slid past him. "Tian's in the kitchen. See you later."

He'd never seen a kitchen like this. Freezer bags, plastic food containers, and food covered every inch. Lots and lots of food. "Expecting an army?"

Tian looked up from the sauce she was ladling over manicotti in a set of containers. "No. This is my once-every-two-months cooking. Breakfast, lunch, and dinners to feed me through most of my flights."

"I thought you were joking in Spokane about taking your food seriously." Chris sat on a barstool that appeared to be the only empty surface.

"This is the first time in a while I've been able to prep this much food. I probably went overboard. Anyway, what would you like for dinner? I've already put the chicken-based dishes in the freezer, but I have some Hawaiian chicken and faux cordon bleu in the fridge. The Manicotti actually needs to freeze before it's edible. I have some kolache-style beef rolls cooking in the oven. And three kinds of muffins…" She looked around the kitchen. "… crust-less mini quiche or breakfast burritos. I am about to package the Oriental chicken and broccoli, but I don't have any rice."

"Wow. So many choices. What is the easiest?"

"Probably the faux cordon bleu." She set down the pan and opened the fridge. "It will just take a minute in the microwave."

"I don't want to eat one of your meals."

"You're not. I made way too much of it. Even with Simone and Brit stealing my meals, it will be too much." Tian took the plate from the microwave. "Sorry, I don't have any sides. I add my fruit and vegetables fresh when I can or buy frozen. Grab a muffin."

Cranberry-orange, or blueberry? The question should be easy. He finally decided on the blueberry. "Aren't you going to eat?"

"I've been taste-testing all day. While you eat, I'll finish packaging the last of this."

With a speed that astounded him, the marble counter and wood tabletop reappeared, while the sink filled with dishes. Tian transferred the smaller items to the dishwasher and filled the sink with water.

"May I help?"

"I didn't ask you to dinner so you can wash dishes."

"I have lots of practice. Javier cooks, I clean, and no one dies of food poisoning."

"Sure, if you want to."

"I'll wash. That way you can dry and put things where you want them."

The smile on her face grew. "You do dishes? I guess you have to be my friend now."

"Hmm." Chris considered making some remark about Javier, but let it pass. "That depends. Do friends get free flights?"

"I receive four friends-and-family passes each year. I gave them all to my aunt because she didn't work for the airlines. But now that she has passed, I'll have to find a new use for them."

"I offer myself as tribute." Chris handed her a ladle, misjudging her grip on the handle, it dropped back into the sink, splashing her.

"Really? You ask for plane tickets and then drench me?" Tian used the ladle to splash water down the front of his shirt. Chris reciprocated with a handful of suds. She grabbed the sink sprayer before he remembered its existence. She got one good shot in, blinding him. He shut off the water at the source rather than grab for the hose. With his other hand, he grabbed the measuring cup out of the suds-filled sink and bailed two scoops at her. Tian shrieked and grabbed his arm. She tried to reach for the water, but he easily blocked her.

"No fair." Her laughter drowned out her protests. He looped his arm around her, and she stepped on his foot as they'd taught in the self-defense class. She exerted no force behind her move, which started him laughing. Still in his arms, she turned, her wet hair slapping his face.

"Oh." Her hand touched his cheek where her hair hit him, and she stopped laughing when their eyes locked. He searched her eyes and lowered his gaze to her lips, then back to her eyes. Had they dilated? Slowly, he lowered his head to meet hers while adjusting his hands to rest at her waist. He didn't want to ruin the moment by asking permission, so he gave her time to run. Tian went up on her tiptoes, bringing her face closer.

"What is going on in here?" Simone's voice caused them both to freeze.

Tian stepped back, and Chris dropped his hands to his side as her roommate entered the kitchen. Simone's eyes took in the damp counters and dripping cupboards, Tian, and ended in the center of his damp shirt. "I guess that is one way to clean the kitchen. I'll leave you to it."

Tian looked down at her wet shirt. Chris turned to the sink so he wouldn't stare.

"I need to change. There is a stack of clean towels on the washer." She pointed to the door hiding their small utility room as she dashed from the kitchen.

Fluffy cumulus clouds! She'd almost kissed him. In her en suite, Tian peeled off her dark green shirt and dried her face and hair. She reminded her reflection of all the reasons Chris should be off limits.

One, his name.

Two, Simone had the worst timing. Wait. Not a reason.

Three… There wasn't a third reason.

She wanted to kiss Chris. There would be little chance of that happening tonight now that Simone had walked in on them. They would both be too conscious of a moment happening again.

Trust. Warmth. Safety.

Double cumulus clouds. Was it possible? She pulled out her blue sweater from the closet and held it to her chest. He-she-never named, Father, and then half a dozen other nameless pilots—all were more than enough reasons not to put trust in another human. And as for feeling safe? Where had that come from? Was a heart ever safe? Could it be?

She pulled the cobalt blue sweater over her head and hurried to the kitchen to clean up.

The kitchen was spotless. Chris stood near the sink with a dish towel over his shoulder.

"That was quick."

"It wasn't as bad as it looked."

"Your shirt is still damp."

"I want to change it, but I also want to share that dessert."

"Your apartment isn't that far. I'll wait."

"Really?"

"Yes, do you want me to heat the brownie?"

"Yes, I'll be back in a moment."

Tian walked him to the door. Before she made it back to the kitchen, Simone came out of her bedroom. "Did I walk in on what I thought I walked in on?"

"What would that be?"

"A kiss." Simone kept her eyes on Tian. "And you are blushing. Tell me."

"Almost."

"I'm so sorry. And now he's gone."

"He's coming back." Tian walked into the kitchen.

"Should I make myself scarce?"

"It doesn't matter." Tian took the brownie from the paper take-out container and set it on a plate in the microwave to reheat. She turned to face Simone. "You know how hard it is to get back those moments. You try too hard, it's never quite right."

"Been there, done that. I feel terrible I ruined your kiss."

"Don't. It gave me a moment to think. My only objection at this point is his name."

"Name, shame, lame?" Simone waved her hands around as if batting the objection away.

A knock at the door interrupted them. Simone rushed back into her bedroom. Tian rolled her eyes and answered the door.

It wasn't Chris. She'd never seen the man holding a bouquet of grocery store flowers before. How had he gotten here? Wasn't security supposed to vet anyone coming up to their floor and message them? Simone had said nothing about expecting a guest. Still, Tian needed to say something "Hi."

"Christian Johnson?" he continued without her acknowledgement. "I'm First Officer Tim Jones. I wanted to say thank you for taking my flight when I thought I needed an appendectomy."

"How did you know where I live?" the nagging question slipped out before anything else—like why he'd only *thought* he needed surgery.

"Your dad told me where you lived—with your cousin Simone." He looked over her shoulder.

Tian stepped into the hall, closing the door behind her, hoping Chris would hurry. Alarm bells rang in Tian's head. She hadn't told her father she was moving. It had never come up during their last flight. She never mentioned Simone to her father. He'd been flying the plane when the incident happened, and there were still hard feelings in his failure to allow the crew to eject the intoxicated man who hit Simone when he got on the plane. Why would this pilot lie? "Flowers weren't necessary. An email would have sufficed."

"I wanted to meet you." He seemed sincere.

Tian forced a smile, wondering what to say next. Chris came around the corner. Relief filled her.

Chris raised a brow but didn't say a word. He waited for her to make the next move. She gave her warmest smile to Chris.

"There you are. This is my boyfriend, Chris, and this is—" Tian didn't fill in the name to show she didn't know the man.

"Tim Jones." He stuck out his hand to shake Chris's.

"He surprised me with flowers to thank me for taking his flight." *Come on, Chris, realize something's wrong.*

Chris shook Tim's hand, and the pilot winced. Behind them, the elevator pinged. Javier and another man wearing the building's security shirt hurried down the hall.

"Anything wrong here?" asked Javier.

Tim stepped back from the three other men. "Nothing. I was giving Christian some flowers. I know her roommate, Simone."

Javier's nose flared. "Did you invite him up?"

"No," said Tian.

"Sir? Can you come with us? Somehow, you missed a security checkpoint, and you are not authorized to be on this floor." Javier and his companion didn't give Tim much of a choice as they crowded him.

Tim thrust the flowers at Tian. She didn't need Chris's head shake to know not to take them. They waited until the elevator closed, leaving only Javier.

Chris set a supportive hand on her back. "What happened?"

"He knocked on the door. I thought it was you. When he mentioned Simone and said my dad told him where I lived, I knew he was lying. My dad doesn't know where I live. Don't ask. And I spoke with Simone in the kitchen. She wasn't expecting anyone."

"Simone is inside?" asked Javier. "May I talk with her?"

Tian used her palm print to let her back into the apartment. "Have a seat. I'll go get her."

Simone answered her knock, and Tian slipped into her cousin's bedroom. "Hey, there was an incident, and Javier wants to talk with you. Nothing big. Chris is here too."

Simone pinched her lips. "He would show up after I took off my makeup."

Tian was sure Simone wasn't talking about Chris. "It will only take a minute, and you look perfect without makeup."

Simone touched the scar near the corner of her left eyebrow and nodded.

Chris and Javier had taken the two chairs, leaving the couch for the women.

"Sorry about this. We denied him access last night. We are going over tape to figure out how he got here. The elevator should have…" Javier stopped his apology. "Tian, tell us what happened."

Tian related the benign interaction. "My dad has no clue where I live, and he and Simone's mom haven't talked in months. Tim had to be lying. Plus, he called me Christian. Even Dad calls me Tian now."

"You are sure your father doesn't know?" asked Javier.

"I'll call and ask him."

Tian dialed her father's number and put it on speaker phone. It was always the safest way to talk with him.

"What's up, peanut? Finally returning my calls?"

Tian cringed. Three untouched voicemails from her father blinked every time she opened her phone. No excuses would justify her ghosting her father since the flight from Boston to Miami that she'd flown for Tim Jones. "Not exactly. Do you know an FO by the name of Tim Jones?"

"Jones… Jones. Yes. Little kid. Not sure how he earned his wings or who passed him to fly an A319. Proof of the pilot shortage."

"Did you tell him where I live?"

"How could I? I only heard you moved out of your crash pad two days ago. And you haven't told me where you went." A sad bitterness laced his voice.

"How did you know I moved?"

"I flew with Draper. Excellent pilot. I told him to tell you and Brit hi. He got a funny look on his face and told me the three of you moved out a couple of weeks ago."

Tian gripped Simone's hand. "Have you said anything to anyone about Simone?"

"Other than legal, no."

"Thanks, Dad. I'll call you later."

"Peanut, I need to know—"

"Dad, please, not now. Bye." She clicked the red end button before her father could respond. "Is that proof enough that Tim lied?"

Chris stared at her.

Tian turned to face Javier. Questions about her less-than-cordial attitude toward her father could wait.

"Yes. Thanks, Tian. Would you two give Simone and me a minute? I need to go over her security plan and figure out how we messed up."

Tian gave Simone's hand a squeeze and went into the kitchen, followed by Chris.

"Did you check your phone before opening the door?"

"I thought it was you."

"You have a high security roommate. You should have checked."

Tian pulled the lukewarm brownie out of the microwave. "I know. I was stupid."

"Hey." Chris touched her arm, spreading enough warmth to reheat the brownie through her. "You aren't stupid. You just forgot to be careful."

Murmured voices came from the other room. If she hadn't opened the door…

"Earth to Tian?" Chris's fingers danced along her arm.

She looked up from the brownie. "Sorry, I was… Here. I don't feel like dessert anymore."

Still facing her, he set the plate on the counter. "We can try for tomorrow."

"It would have to be earlier. I need to leave for the airport at 7 am on Friday."

"That's right. The pilot gets to fly to exotic places."

"Not really. I need twenty-five more 787 flight hours before February 16. I don't have enough seniority to fly to the cool places often."

"I'm not sure what that means."

"Just because I am a pilot doesn't mean that I can fly any plane I want to. Pilots have to learn and certify each jet. Once we're trained, then we need to fly one hundred hours in that type of plane within one hundred days. The 787/747 class is used for long flights, the ones overseas. Once I finish my certification, then I go back to flying my regular routes. Few of them are exotic. I mean Boise is nice but not exotic at all. In another ten or fifteen years, I'll fly to more fun places."

"Did you dis Boise?"

"Never. Every town I've flown to has its own adventure."

"So tomorrow?" Chris turned his head to the doorway.

Javier stepped into the kitchen. "Simone is going to come down to the office with me."

Tian waited for the apartment door to close before speaking. Realizing they were alone, her body reacted most irrationally and her stomach rumbled. "I guess I got my appetite back."

"Then what are we waiting for?" Chris reached behind her and put the brownie back in the microwave.

Fifteen seconds was all it took for the brownie to heat. Fifteen of the longest seconds known to man. Chris spent all of them wondering if she would accept his kiss. He leaned forward, and her lips parted as the microwave dinged. The single beep was all it took to break the spell pulling them together. Tian spun out of his arms and into action, retrieving the ice cream from her freezer.

Had he been reading her wrong?

Tian got out two spoons. At least she wasn't dividing the dessert into two bowls. They sat at the bar and shared the brownie.

"This is amazing! I was disappointed it didn't come with chocolate sauce, but this brownie doesn't need it." Tian turned her spoon over in her mouth to clean it off.

How was he not supposed to think of kissing her now? "If you think this is good, you should have it straight out of the oven."

"If that is an invitation—yes."

"And they say the way to a man's heart is through his stomach."

"This isn't food, it's ambrosia." She took another bite, leaving him with the last one.

He lifted the plate and used his spoon to point to her. Tian shook her head, Chris took the last gooey bite.

Tian set down her spoon and watched him. "You have a little above your lip."

Chris tried to lick it off, which made her giggle.

"No right here." She touched the spot with her finger. Chris froze as she slipped off her stool and stood before him, her finger still at the corner of his mouth. Standing next to him while he sat on the stool put their eyes at the same level. As she dropped her hand onto his shoulder, her mouth curved into a smile. Her light touch pinned him in place more solidly than he had ever been pinned on a sparring mat. Her eyes flitted to his, then to his mouth.

She leaned forward and pressed her lips to his. She tasted of brownies and something sweeter. Chris placed a hand on her hip, hoping she'd stay long enough for him to figure it out. Tian lifted her head a mere inch, ending the kiss. "Better than the brownie."

"Are you sure?" Chris urged her closer and captured her lips again. He kept the kiss light, letting her lead. They hadn't gone on a real date yet.

This time, when she pulled back, she stepped away, dropping her hand to his arm. Chris removed his hand from her hip, wondering what would happen next. He would not apologize and she better not either.

"I don't usually... not on the first... or is it second..."

Chris raised a finger to her lips to stop her from stammering. "I didn't think you did. But please don't regret it."

She straightened. "I don't. And I would do it again."

"Really?"

She blushed deeply. "I mean first kiss with you."

"A few minutes ago, you called me your boyfriend. I know it was to warn that guy off..."

"I don't do casual or meaningless, despite my career stereotype."

"I know." Chris ran his hand down her arm, stopping when he intertwined his fingers with hers. "And I don't like to play games. As far as I'm concerned, we started something that has commitment in it."

Her eyes widened.

"Girlfriend." Chris tugged her hand, pulling her into another kiss.

Eleven

TIAN SPENT DAYS PLANNING HER next forty-eight hours. The last time she'd been in Hawaii, she'd just graduated from high school. Dad had taken her as a graduation present. He'd spent most of the week entertaining wife-to-never-be while leaving Tian to explore on her own. So she'd already seen the Pearl Harbor National Memorial. Last time, she'd been intrigued with the ads for the Polynesian Cultural Center on the north end of the island. Instead, her father had taken her to a luau run by the hotel. He'd disappeared halfway through, leaving her to fend off the advances of more than one man.

The long uneventful flight left her more than a little tired. The shuttle van waited to take her and the other two pilots to the hotel. The flight attendants had already left, most likely for a different hotel. Tian didn't mind that she would spend much of the next day and a half on her own. Growing up the way she had made her either independent, introverted, or a loner, depending on who described her. Fortunately, she'd had enough sense of adventure to experience what she could when it was offered. Hotel rooms, with a few exceptions, were rarely meant to be enjoyed for more than their utility. She claimed her key and found her room. Not surprising, it had no view of the ocean; however it was clean and cheery, and thankfully showed no signs of bedbugs.

She changed into her swimsuit, basketball shorts, and a t-shirt. A lava-lava for herself and chocolate-covered macadamia nuts for her roommates were the only two purchases she planned to make on the island. She might add a third if she found something for Chris. A hula girl for his dashboard was fun and flirty. She opened her phone.

> Tian: Landed and settled in. No coat needed. Heading to the beach.

She added a smiling sun emoji and copied the message to her mother, Chris, and the group chat with Simone and Brit.

Her mother responded first.

> Mom: Glad you made it. Will you please call your father? He resorted to sending me an email.
> Tian: I talked to him on Wednesday.
> Mom: Please.
> Tian: Fine.

Tian opened a conversation with her father. His Merry Christmas wish to her was still on the screen. Above it was a single plea to call him. She still hadn't listened to the three voicemails he'd left earlier. She sent a return text.

> Tian: I am in Hawaii. I like the 787. I'll be around all evening if you want to call.

From the side pocket of her suitcase, she pulled out a clear plastic zipper bag and dropped her phone inside. Reading novels on a phone app around sand and water required diligence—the perfect job for the quart bag required for TSA security. The only thing Tian lacked was a beach towel, which could be picked up at any number of tourist shops near the hotel. She double-checked that she had her key card, and her phone rang. A number she didn't recognize.

"Hello?"

"Hi, peanut."

Dad. "I didn't recognize the number."

"My battery is almost dead. I'm calling you from my hotel phone. I'm in LA."

"Oh." More likely, he hoped she'd answer an unknown number.

"I have something important to ask you, and I want you to think about it. Can you give me five minutes?" Something in his voice sounded desperate.

"Sure." The bed sank as she sat on its side.

"You are getting your hours on the 787, right?"

"Yes."

"I want you to be my FO on my flight to Paris on February 13th and return on the 16th."

"Why?"

"Because it will be my last flight." He paused. "I'm retiring."

"What? You are only fifty-five."

"-six."

"Why?"

"My last medical exam didn't go so well. They found cancer. Early stages."

"Wait—should you be flying? Shouldn't you have chemo or something?"

"Starting February 20th."

A lump formed in her throat. She hadn't been close to her father for years. No reason to be this emotional about someone she'd already lost. "What about flying?"

"I need to work through my next anniversary with the airlines before I retire. Your grandfather will get his wish that I take a position on the board."

Valentine's Day. Her father often mentioned his hire date was meant to be. "Is it safe for you to fly?"

"Yes. I am taking a lighter schedule. I fly back to Boston in the morning. Then I'll take two weeks of vacation until our Paris flight."

He referred to the flight as theirs, although she hadn't answered him.

"I'll go with you on one condition: if you are not well enough, you won't fly."

"I would never put a flight in danger."

Tian wondered how sincere the answer was. Had he told the airline? Did she have an obligation to? She pushed that question out of her mind for now. "Does my mom know?"

"I told her two days ago."

"What about Brit?"

"I wanted to talk to you first."

"What about Simone? And legal?"

"I'm taking care of that." Translation, none of her business.

With all of the practical questions out of the way, she asked, "How long?"

"Until I die? Probably years. Until the treatment is over? I'll know better after this round of chemo. Hopefully, in less than six months."

"Are you in pain?"

"No."

"Anything I can do?"

"Just agree to fly to Paris with me."

"Yes. What about the arrangements with scheduling?" Tian could put in a request for a Paris flight and with the needed hours, she was likely to be assigned a Paris flight; however, the timing would be up to someone else.

"Make sure you request Paris to finish out your hours."

"I will." Tian gulped. As a child, she had no problem saying I love you to her parents. The little girl in her wanted to say those words now, but would he believe them? Would she? "Thank you for inviting me on your last flight. I know it will be special."

"I'm so proud of you, peanut. Thanks. I'll let you know when it is arranged." The line went silent.

Tian stared at her phone screen. Cancer. Brit would not handle this well. Simone and Brit's boyfriend would be there for Brit.

She'd have to wait until Brit said something.

She texted her mom.

> Tian: Dad gave me a lot to process.
>
> Mom: Kurt has always been the go-big-or-go-home type. Are you okay?
>
> Tian: I will be. I wish I had forgiven him before now.
>
> Mom: You still have time. He is likely to recover from this with treatment.
>
> Tian: I want to, but now I am bitter that he just ruined Hawaii.
>
> Mom: You could have called him back sooner.
>
> Tian: So I ruined Hawaii?
>
> Mom: Only a volcano could do that. You can choose to enjoy your time or not.

Tian wanted to scream, not listen to her mother's "life is what you make of it" speech.

Her phone pinged.

> Chris: Beach? I have a beach. Only it is covered with snow and ice.

That conversation looked like it could be more fun. Tian finished her conversation with her mother first.

> Tian: I see your point. I meant I would worry about him. He said he was going back to Boston. Does he still have his place? I thought the current wife was in Atlanta.
>
> Mom: She left him months ago. Divorce is final. He is going to live in my spare room.

Tian stared at the screen. Her parents were living together again?

> Mom: Close your mouth. I can hear you yelling from here. After everything, we've stayed friends. He can't go stay with his parents because of their health, but here he will be close to them. Your aunt's old room will work for him when the time comes.

The room that contained a hospital bed and smelled like death? It had been mostly empty at the funeral. This was what Mom got for turning in her flight attendant uniform for nurses' scrubs. Now every relative that needed hospice…

> Tian: I'm shocked but not surprised. You are the nicest person on earth.

> Mom: It took me a couple of days to offer. I also think it will be good for you and Brit to have a place to come see him over the next few months.

Further proof that her mother deserved sainthood. How many women would take in their ex-husband's daughter, who happened to be born while they were still married? Only Mom. The best part of that extraordinary mess was she'd gotten a sister out of the deal.

> Tian: You are the best. It must be late there. Love you.

Finally, free to leave her room, Tian texted Chris as she walked down the hall.

> Tian: If it makes you feel better, I haven't made it to the beach yet.

It took long enough for Tian to respond to his text. Chris wondered if she'd been surfing.

> Chris: Doesn't. I pictured you having fun.

> Tian: I am on my way to a souvenir shop now to buy a cheap towel and maybe a lava-lava.

> Chris: You don't strike me as they type to purchase a lot of souvenirs.

> Tian: Other than bears…Which most of them have been for occasions, not places. I usually bring Brit and Simone the local chocolate specialty. How was your day?

Chris: Boring. The way I like it. Can we call?

Tian: Let me put in some earbuds. One minute.

Chris: Call when ready.

Chris picked up on the first ring. "Hey. Was your flight good?"

"Standard. The landing was a little nerve-racking—new airport, big plane, worried I'd mess up."

"Which you must have done perfectly since there is nothing on the TV about a plane crash in Hawaii."

"My goal in life is to not mess up to the point that anyone uses the recording as a lesson on YouTube or mocks me on Twitter or TikTok."

"Mine is to not be in the news."

"So our career goals are the same. Yet another thing we have in common. We want the day to be as uneventful as possible."

Chris couldn't help but laugh. "So boring is good?"

"So we're a boring couple?" Her voice held no laughter.

"I meant it as a joke."

"I know. Sorry. I just —" She paused.

Chris wondered if Tian was crying.

"—give me a second to go back to my room… I'll explain. Oh, and tell me something funny."

It was one of those moments when one knows a thousand funny things have happened, but they can't find anything funny. "When I was five, I lost both my front teeth at the same time, and my brother kept making me say my name. Not funny, I know, but it is the best I am coming up with. Once when I was on a hospital visit with Mrs. Ogilvie, a kid asked me if I was one of the people they show on TV with the President. I once told a high school guidance counselor I wanted to be a stand-up comedian. Good thing he talked me out of it."

Finally, a laugh. Followed by a sob and a door shutting. "Thanks. I needed that."

"What is wrong?"

"My father called…" Tian described a conversation she'd had with her father and the dreaded C word.

Chris waited until she finished. "I gathered the other night that you and your father don't speak much."

"For my twelfth birthday, my dad gave me Brit. And asked my mother for a divorce, because Brit's mom needed to be on his health insurance. I love Brit, but most teenage girls don't want a nine-year-old surprise. Mom had suspected that Dad wasn't faithful. Brit's mom thought she was married to my dad all along. So it was kind of a mess. After her mother died, Brit came and lived with us permanently. I was a sophomore in high school by then. Mom had three years to drill into me I couldn't blame Brit or her mom, so I took all my emotions out on Dad. It didn't help that he moved on to wife number three and I gained a brother."

"Wow, I can see why you would be angry." Chris thought it best to keep listening.

"Since then, six women I know of have claimed to have children with him. Only two of them stood up to paternity tests. Wife three left him, of course. I assume in four or five more years, Brit and I will hear from our brother again. It is seriously messed up. Mom said number four just left him. I have twin half-brothers from her."

"And your mom is taking care of him?" Chris repeated what she'd told him earlier, still not quite believing.

"Yup, that is my mom. If we were Catholic, I'd petition the Vatican to make her a saint. I don't understand how they are still friends or how she can still like him."

"I can."

"What?"

Chris hadn't meant to say that. It was too early in the relation-ship to have a tell-all, especially when she was a jillion miles away. He took a deep breath. "Two days before my wedding, I got a phone call from my best man. He asked me to meet him at an address. Long story short was I found my bride with a mutual friend…” The story was hard to tell. “They were only wearing their birthday suits and you can guess the rest.”

“Oy, that is bad.”

“I felt betrayed, obviously, but I still don’t hate her. I wouldn’t get involved with her again, but if she were in a situation where she needed my professional help, I could work with her.”

“How?”

“She had, and still has, many good qualities. And she had some bad ones. Like flirting with anything that breathes. I didn’t see that at the time. My friend had tried to warn me. Your mom knew your dad for a lot longer than I knew my ex. Still, we have some mutual friends, so for everyone’s sake, including mine, I decided to not make it a bigger deal. Anyway, I can understand how your parents could be friends.”

“But aren’t you furious?”

“At the time I was. Looking back, I’m glad we didn’t marry. Sorry, this is not a conversation for only a few days into knowing each other…” Chris pulled back the curtains on his window and looked over the Chicago lights. “There is so much hate in the world; I don’t want to contribute.”

The silence from the other end of the line continued long enough he wondered if they had disconnected; however, muffled sounds still came through the line, crescendoing into sobs. Crying women always made situations awkward. A crying woman on the other end of a phone line amped that up. Hugging was out, teasing a smile was out, waiting for a response was out, and there was zero chance at this point she’d change to a video call.

“Tian?”

“I…I’m fine. So. Much. Call. Later. Bye.” The line went dead.

He rested his head against the cool glass of the window. A new record. Three days from first kiss to the beginning of the end.

Twelve

THE BEST PART OF HAWAII was the number of distractions it offered. Tian kept most of her sightseeing plans in place. Reading on the beach didn't happen. The beach part did, just not the reading—which was replaced by soul searching. Over the years, Dad had gone out of his way to be there for both her and Brit like graduations, her first flight, and sometime during the Christmas season. He'd only stepped back after Tian had told him to take a long taxi off a short runway, metaphorically speaking, of course. He was the only person close to her who understood the thrill of looking out of the cockpit window. The one dream he'd always shared with her. Even as a child, Brit, with her thick glasses perched on her nose, never wanted to be a pilot. Which was just as well since she only passed her driver's license eye test with one eye.

The entire love/hate relationship she had with nepotism was largely on Dad and Grandpa. She appreciated all they did to smooth her path to becoming a commercial pilot without any school debt. So many pilots had to take out loans for school and to fulfill their flight hours. She'd skipped all of that at the cost of every pilot at Legacy Air knowing that she was fast-tracked into the company and suspecting that she wasn't a good pilot.

Which all boiled down to Tian spending every hour she wasn't worried about her father, working to get the remaining hours in on the 787 and wondering how many of the regular pilots would add extra tests or lectures to her skills. She always appreciated the input, but an hour lecture on a particular plane's feature was, more often than not, overkill.

Somehow in between, she fit in worrying about Simone, Brit, and her phone call with Chris, which resulted in her purchasing not one but two boxes of chocolate-covered macadamia nuts for each person—because she'd eaten the first set.

So when the captain asked her to take the controls for the landing at O'Hare, she shouldn't have been surprised. A predawn landing in lightly falling snow, with 305 souls on board, with two experienced pilots watching every move, it was the experience she needed. Thankfully, everything went simulator-perfect. Even her favorite air traffic controller was working the radio.

The captain gathered his things. "Tian, I'd heard that you were an excellent pilot, but having flown with your dad, grandfather, and then, once I met your great grandfather, I had my doubts. I figured they would have pulled some strings. You put those fears to rest. I'd be glad to fly with you anytime."

"Thank you."

"I second that. I've flown with some others from the founding families—Johnsons, Pitts, Hansons, Carvers—and not all of them have been up to standards," said the other pilot.

Tian felt a blush rising. Three of the four founding members of Legacy were flyers. Their descendants and other relatives represented nearly ten percent of the airline's employees, most of them part of the nine thousand pilots that flew for the airline. "I appreciate you letting me land at my home airport."

The captain laughed. "Next time, we'll make it harder."

Likely there wouldn't be a next time. Schedules on the 787s went to those with more seniority.

Brit waited for her at the end of the jetway. She didn't wear any makeup and her eyes were red. "Do you have time for breakfast? My shift doesn't start until ten."

"Sure. Give me a few minutes. I'll meet you?"

"Berghoff Restaurant. Simone is already there."

Of course. Hands down best breakfast at the airport. Tian debated her omelet choices on the walk over.

At the far back, Simone sat with Brit and three plates.

"We ordered your favorite omelet. Hope you don't mind. I only have an hour before I need to be at work." Simone looked much more composed than Brit had.

Not disappointed at their choice, Tian sat in the empty chair. "Did Dad call?"

Brit sniffled. "Late last night. He wants us to be on the Paris flight with you."

"Both of you? Are you going to be?"

"We have complimentary seats. Perk of the last flight. He can take guests. I had no idea there was such a policy." Simone sipped her hot chocolate. "He apologized."

"What?" Tian's fork fell to her plate. Those were two words she never thought she would hear about her father.

"Told me he should have dealt with the passenger differently. Hindsight is 20/20 right? Yes, the guy was a bit sauced when he boarded, but we've had worse. If we started denying every tipsy passenger, we'd kick off enough fares to make the airport bars complain. And if we kicked off every person who made a pass at a 'stewardess'"—she used air quotes— "the pilot shortage would be a whole lot worse."

"It is not that bad, is it?"

Simone set her cup down. "No. I've only had a couple of pilots make passes. From what my mom says, the 60s and 70s were a lot worse. Sorry, I am not in the best mood."

Tian laid her fork down. "None of us are in a good mood. I am still not sure how to react to Dad's news. Every New Year's, I've put 'mend bridges with Dad' on my resolution list, mostly at

Mom's request. Now I feel like I'm running out of time even if Dad says he'll be around for years."

"You've always been the angriest at him. Why?" asked Brit.

"I'm not sure. Maybe it was that I was in my teenage angst years when everything happened. All of a sudden I had a sister—whom I adore—but I felt like I wasn't good enough, so he needed another daughter. I think that is when I started having to prove myself. Pilot's license earned the first day I was eligible. Valedictorian, you bet. The harder I tried, the more attention he spent elsewhere. Oh, here is wife number three. Mind if I bring her to graduation? But at the same time, he was always there. Something I took for granted."

Simone touched Tian's shoulder. "You spent the entire weekend rehashing the last fifteen years, didn't you?"

Tian nodded.

"Stop. Just stop. Think about the future. You have time with your dad. Take it. Do you want to forgive him?" Brit's question brought one word to mind.

"Yes."

"Then do it. Sort out the rest of the emotions later."

So simple.

"Brit, what did I ever do to get a sister like you?" Tian blinked back a tear.

"Nothing, that is all on Dad."

They all laughed.

A phone pinged, and they all automatically checked theirs. Tian discovered hers was still in airplane mode. She turned it on.

Simone gasped. "Listen to this, it is from the legal team. The civil suit against the airlines has been dropped, and they banned the guy from Legacy Air for five years. I was hoping for life, but I'll take it. This means I can return to a flight crew…Maybe…Oh, it is a crazy idea. What if I got on the crew for the Paris flight?"

Tian's phone vibrated in her hand as alert after alert downloaded.

"That's brilliant." Brit tapped her chin. "Can you put in a good word for me for your job? I'd rather organize pilot schedules than what I am doing now. I'm so tired of hearing passengers' lies and sob stories."

"I didn't know you were looking for a change."

"I've been thinking about it. I check the employee website every week to see if something I'd like has been posted."

The phone finished vibrating and Tian looked to see what she missed. The first message that caught her eye was from Chris offering to drive her home.

She responded: Yes. I'll be ready in fifteen minutes.

The answer to the last of several texts had been worth waiting for. Chris pulled out of the general aviation lot at Chicago Executive Airport. Candace and her friends had left for New York an hour ago. Since Abbie, Mandy Crawford, and Kimberly Hastings, Alex's wife, were traveling together, the protection teams were consolidated and combined with those from Dermott Security, leaving Chris and several other Hastings employees with a light load for the rest of the week.

Today he didn't have another duty until early in the afternoon when the elementary school let out for the day.

He reached O'Hare before he realized he did not know where to pick Tian up. He told his phone to call her.

She picked up on the second ring.

"Hi, where do I pick you up?"

"Oh, I'm not at my terminal. Terminal one, lower level. I'll be the one with the white pilot hat on."

The hat and pilot's jacket did indeed make her easy to spot. He pulled to the curb and hopped out to help her with her bag. "Aren't you freezing?"

"Yes, but I didn't want to take my coat with me. Warm car to warm airport didn't require an extra warm coat. Thanks for the lift, and sorry we never got back to talking."

He closed the passenger door behind her and hurried around to his side before an airport employee could yell at him for not staying in his vehicle. "Not your fault. Every time one of us was free, the other wasn't."

"Your advice helped me look at the situation in a different way. I called Dad again and agreed to meet to talk with him. You're sure you didn't miss your calling in life to be a therapist?"

The compliment warmed him. "School was always difficult for me. The thought of college terrified me. The academy was enough."

"You have talent, though."

Chris reached for her hand and gave it a caress before returning both hands to the wheel. Driving in Chicago traffic during falling snow wasn't the best place to hold hands. "Tell me about what you got to see."

Tian launched into a travel log which was perfect for the drive to their apartment building. Chris concentrated on the road without being required to answer often. As they exited the freeway, the snow stopped falling. "When is your next flight?"

"Today is Monday, right?" She yawned.

Chris smiled but didn't laugh. "Yes."

She counted on her fingers. "I think it is Thursday. I could check my phone, but it is too much effort. I need to take a nap. Wow, that hit fast."

"I guess pilots don't sleep on planes."

"Yes and no. Since the flight is over eight hours, we had a three-pilot crew, so we rotate. We all had to be in the cockpit for takeoff and landing, but then we each had a rest period. And we have a bed. I laid down but didn't sleep very well. I'm not used to sleeping on a flight."

"So, I guess asking you to lunch is out."

She checked her watch. "I am planning on taking a nap until three-ish. Can you do an early dinner?"

"Not today. I'm on duty from a half an hour before school gets out through about eight o'clock. Maybe dessert?"

"I don't want to eat that late. How about something else?"

"I'll text when I'm done, then?" He pulled into the underground garage.

"That works. Are you doing the personal safety class again tomorrow?"

"I'm on schedule—"

"We could make that a date."

Chris pulled into his space. "I wish. I am on duty before and after. How about a late breakfast tomorrow?"

Tian sighed. "Dad is flying in to do some paperwork at the main offices. I was going to meet him."

"What about Wednesday lunch?"

"Yes. I can do lunch on Wednesday."

He'd take what he could get. Obviously, they needed to plan ahead if they were going to spend time together. "May I walk you to your door?"

"Then you can keep me from falling asleep in the elevator."

It had been too many days since he'd held her. Kissing always made him more alert. "I am sure I can keep you awake."

"Really?" She yawned again. "I'm sure the building has policies against jumping in elevators, and I know there is a security camera."

Chris wrapped one arm around her waist. "I could find out if you are ticklish."

"Then I'd scream, and Javier would rush to see what the problem was... Too messy."

He brought his lips to her ear. "I could whisper jokes in your ear and make you giggle. Then Javier would just have to wonder."

She leaned against his shoulder. "I think I am too tired to giggle."

"Then I'll keep you upright." Some days the express elevator was too quick. Chris wheeled Tian's bag to her door, and she brushed a kiss on his cheek. He would have liked more, but as tired as she was, it would have been a disservice.

Thirteen

To give them privacy, Tian invited her father to the apartment for lunch. After eating a meal where they mostly reminisced and caught up, they retired to the living room.

"This is such a nice place. How could you afford it?"

"Simone qualified for a special grant because of her media attention after she was attacked on the plane. We had some fears that the hundredth anniversary articles would spawn some attention to all three of us. But it's been mostly positive."

"How is Simone?"

"Hopeful to get back on a cabin crew. She thinks with yesterday's news that she can."

"She'd be safer on long-haul flights. In business or first class," said her father.

"I don't think she has the seniority for that."

"Legacy has a duty to all of their employees to keep them safe."

Tian did a double take. This was so far from his original comments to Simone about being a whiner and ignoring passes from passengers. "She said you apologized."

"I even called myself a male chauvinist pig." Her father chuckled. "It took me a long time to grow up. I understand now why my last two wives divorced me. Until the diagnosis, I didn't realize that I was not twenty-seven anymore. I'd say I regretted it all, but I love Brit too much. I can't regret her. My middle son will never see me again. Ex number three's husband asked to legally adopt him, and I gave my consent. And the twins are apparently not mine after all. So now you have only one step sibling you'll ever know." He didn't mention the children from the paternity suits. As far as Tian knew, the settlements all included that he had no contact with the children.

"I've always wondered about how you balanced two families for so long."

"Mostly stupid luck. When you were little, your mother and I tried to keep separate schedules so at least one of us was home each night. That made it easy to start with. Then your mom got her RN. She knew I was, in her words, 'messing around.' Brit's mom did too. The week after Brit's mom died, your mother told me she'd known for years. Boston is a big place, but not big enough. Your mothers met in a yoga class two or three years before Brit's mom got sick. Taking in Brit was your mother's idea. She reasoned correctly that I'd be more likely to be involved in your lives, and it was better than Brit having to move to Nevada and live with an uncle she'd never met."

"Why didn't Mom tell me that?" Misplaced anger rumbled through Tian, looking for an escape route.

"Your mother had her reasons. I know the entire situation was messed up. It was my mess-up. And you have every right to be upset with me."

"I want to forgive you. But it is hard. I've been angry for so long. And I know you have tried. You never missed a single birthday. But then I fly with one of the older pilots and they realize I'm yours, and…"

"And you have to face my reputation."

"Yup. There is that."

"Have you ever thought about leaving Legacy?"

"And break Grandpa's heart?"

"It wouldn't break his heart. He only wants you to be happy. Yes, he was thrilled to have a granddaughter earn her wings, but he wouldn't care if all you ever flew was his Cessna on weekend trips."

"I thought the whole four generation thing…"

"Is a cool perk. But he doesn't want to dictate your future."

"I love to fly. No one made that choice for me."

"But it doesn't have to be Legacy Air. There may be a day when you want to look at flying corporate or cargo that keeps you on a more regular schedule and closer to home. A pilot's life is hard on relationships and families—even when the pilot isn't a jerk like me and only has one family, which he is faithful to. And, yes, there are a lot of them out there."

"I've never considered leaving Legacy."

"Honestly, the best job I had was being a dad. I blew it spectacularly. Infidelity aside, I'd do a lot of things differently if I could do it all over. Those years before 9-11, when your mom and I both still flew, even though we tried to arrange our schedules so one of us was home, it meant we rarely saw each other, and you spent a lot of time with Aunt Ella. When neither of us could reach home to be with you for four days, that was the worst. My point is, someday you may want a family and Legacy Air shouldn't be more important than your spouse and children."

"I'm hoping with the new maternity leave policies, it would be easier to stay."

"One time that nepotism pays. Your Aunt Jenny campaigned for years for the flight attendants. When she pointed out that pilots had it worse, she got changes made there as well."

"Back to whatever the point was, because I am sure this isn't about my fictitious future."

"Sorry. I've been thinking about all the things I'll miss. Grandchildren came up in that list."

Tian didn't comment. Children were not on her radar. A second date was as far as she could consider. "Dad, you said you would be fine."

"And I will be. I've just been thinking of my own mortality. I guess it comes with hearing the doctor say 'cancer.'"

"I'm glad I told you I forgive you…" Tears filled her eyes.

"It wouldn't have mattered to me." He pulled her into a hug.

Memories of her childhood flooded her. She should have forgiven him years ago.

Chris arrived at Hastings seconds before the class began. This week, ZoElle led the class. Dana and a female he didn't know demonstrated. Chris helped several of the class members work through a slow-motion purse snatching scenario before turning them loose on the sparring dummy. Like last week, Tian worked with Alex Hastings. Chris tried to catch her eye a couple of times and failed. She seemed quiet. Had something gone wrong with her father?

Near the end of the class, Allie and Melanie joined them, mostly observing.

When class ended, he went to talk to Tian only to see she was deep in conversation with Melanie. He waved before running out the door to his next assignment. Since another bodyguard drove, he snuck in a quick text.

> Chris: R U ok? Sorry I didn't have time to talk. See you tomorrow morning. Does 8 work?

They reached the venue, and she hadn't answered.

> Chris: I'm on phone silence for the next five hours. I'll text later.

The event would be over before then, but cleanup could last for hours.

"Johnson, start with the caterers," Alan Hastings's voice came clear through in his earpiece.

"Will do."

Everything went smoothly. Five hours later, Chris headed home for the night with a nice to-go box from catering. Hastings had some of the best clients. This one insisted that since they paid the caterers for the food, they could divide leftovers as they wished among the staff, including security. Chris secretly believed they over-ordered deliberately. The catering staff had leftovers, too. Riding in the back of the SUV, he opened his phone.

> Tian: I'm fine. It was a deep talk. Breakfast sounds good. Text when you are off.

> Chris: Headed back now are you still awake?

> Tian: Barely. I turn into a pumpkin at 10. I know. I feel so old.

> Chris: Nothing wrong with a good night's sleep.

> Tian: I could use a hug, though.

> Chris: We could go up to the atrium.

> Tian: The what?

> Chris: Best view of the city. Also one of the better-kept secrets in the building.

> Tian: Sounds good.

> Chris: Be there in 20.

He made it in seventeen minutes.

Tian opened the door seconds after his knock. Her eyelids drooped slightly. It took him a moment to realize her face was devoid of makeup. Without preamble, she walked into his arms for her hug. He held her tight and kissed the top of her head.

"Let me show you the atrium." He slid his arm around her waist and led her to the elevator and up to the floor above the small gym and pool. Most of the east side of the building was encased in glass, creating a greenhouse of sorts filled with potted trees and plants. Cushioned furniture lay scattered in conversation groups.

Tian looked up through the windows into the evening darkness. Low cloud cover reflected the city's lights instead of stars. "This is amazing. It wasn't in the brochures or the tour."

"It is a low-impact area, limited to the residents on the security floors, providing they find it." He led her to a set of chairs nestled behind a row of potted shrubs. "This spot is blind to the cameras."

A soft laugh escaped her lips. "I hadn't thought about cameras. Isn't it dangerous to have a blind spot?"

"They designed it this way. Security can see who enters the area and who leaves. As long as people enter willingly, we leave them alone. When Colin Ogilvie was a newlywed, he wanted some private spots."

"So Javier and everyone else know we are here and assume…?"

"That we want a private conversation." Chris settled into an oversized chair and put his feet up on an ottoman. The seat was not big enough to call a sofa, yet large enough to hold two. "Tell me about your day."

Tian tucked herself into his side. "Lunch was interesting."

"With your dad?"

"Yes." She gave him several details of the conversation. "I forgave him."

Chris held her hand, tracing invisible patterns on her wrist. "How do you feel about the rest of his visit?"

"Peaceful. I thought it would take longer to shed the anger—maybe because I had all weekend to prepare. I kept thinking about you and your ex. Thank you for sharing." She turned, settling her head into his shoulder and moving the hand he held to his chest.

A comfortable, warm silence encompassed them. Contented, Chris leaned his head on top of hers and watched out the window. A change in Tian's breathing alerted him to her sleeping state. They'd barely known each other for two weeks, and she trusted him enough to fall asleep in his arms with no makeup. Chris supposed that most men wouldn't find the combination attractive. To him, it signaled trust. A trust he never believed could happen after their first meeting. He'd dated his ex for months before he felt this comfortable with her. He closed his eyes and let his mind wander to the possibilities of a future.

Fourteen

"Excuse me. Excuse me." The words should not be coming from the cockpit readout. "Excuse me."

"Get lost." Chris's voice rumbled beneath Tian's ear.

Tian's pillow moved, and she blinked herself awake. Her pillow growled. It only took a second to realize that her pillow had a heartbeat and a name. Chris. They must have fallen asleep.

A man in a security guard uniform stood a few feet away. "Sorry to wake you, but you shouldn't be sleeping here."

Tian lifted her head, and Chris sat up. "We are awake. And we'll leave."

"Sorry, I am to escort you out. It is 1:00 a.m. and the atrium is closed for its nightly cleaning."

Tian rose on shaky feet.

Chris was immediately beside her with a hand on her back. "Thanks, Nash. I'm sure we can find the door."

They crossed the atrium ahead of the security guard. Once outside the door, Chris steered her to the elevator. The guard didn't follow.

The black eye of the elevator's security camera stared down at them. In her foggy mind, Tian realized they were once again being watched. She giggled.

"Tired much?"

She pointed to the camera. "I realized that Javier will probably hear about your four hours in the camera-free zone and assume." Tian ran a hand through her unruly hair. "I think I am overtired."

The elevator stopped at their floor. Chris took her hand and led her off. "That is one downside of Two Garden Tower. No making out in the stairwell."

At her door, Tian rose on her toes and kissed him lightly. "One of these days. we'll have to visit the atrium again." She turned to the camera and blew a kiss, followed by a wave.

"Should I be jealous that they got a kiss, too?"

"I wanted them to know I knew they were there."

Chris moved between her and the hallway camera. "Most likely they aren't paying attention to this camera, anyway."

"Then I can give you a better goodnight kiss." Tian set her hands on his shoulders.

Chris grinned as he lowered his head to meet hers.

Conscious of the camera, Tian kept the kiss short and sweet. "Breakfast tomorrow?"

"Definitely."

Chris squinted at his ringing phone before answering the pre 5:00 a.m. call. The Hastings dispatcher's voice was far too cheery as he described the situation and the need for Chris to switch shifts because of illness. He'd end up pulling a double today.

He waited until he was in the elevator to text Tian, hoping to not wake her with the bad news.

Chris: Called in to work. Raincheck? Likely working back-to-
back shifts.

Several hours later, he found a moment to check his phone for messages.

Tian: Bummer.

Tian: Took myself out to breakfast. Had the best Monte Cristo of my life.

Tian: I have a 5 a.m. report time tomorrow. Goal is to go to bed by 9 at the latest. When do you get off?

Chris: If I am lucky, I can be back by 2030. I mean 8:30.

Tian: I'm a pilot. I know military time…another thing we have in common. I also use Zulu. ;)

Her immediate answer meant they had a couple minutes for conversation. Even if it was about time zones or the time in Greenwich, England. He understood why using Zulu or Coordinated Universal Time (UTC) avoided confusion arising from local time differences for pilots.

Chris: Zulu is too much math, but I am usually in the central time zone anyway. I get confused when I eat lunch at dinner time.

Tian: There is that. Hope to see you tonight.

Chris: Me too.

It was after ten when he finally ended his day.

Chris: Sorry.

No response came to his text, not that he expected one. He woke up to a text from Tian.

Tian: I should end up in Denver tonight. Maybe we can call.

Staring at the phone screen, Chris understood his former girlfriend's frustration with his job. Tian's offered an entire new set of obstacles. A long-distance relationship with a local zip code. He knew better than to believe his schedule would improve over the years. Being on a dedicated crew was only as normal as the principal's life. In the summer, he could end up anywhere the Ogilvies traveled, or he could end up in Japan next time Colin had an innovative idea. If he could make his off days line up with Tian's it would be better.

His phone pinged. Hastings. Aligning workdays would not happen soon.

Denver International, DEN, ranked as super-saver economy in Tian's ranking of airports. She shouldn't lay her finger on the reason she thought that. Perhaps it was because Grandpa used the old acronym, DIA, that he claimed stood for Darn Inconvenient Airport so many times. Or it was the fact that they ended up in a hotel in suburbia with nothing nearby to explore. After completing her bedbug check, she heated her dinner and texted Chris.

Tian: In Denver. An Air Force Falcon flew with us today.

Twenty minutes later, her phone pinged an answer.

Chris: How did you fly a military plane?

Tian: I didn't. A falcon, a bird with feathers, flew on the plane.
There are jets called Falcons, but I haven't flown one.

Chris: You had a bird as a passenger?

Tian: Yup.

She attached the photo of the Air Force Cadet holding the hooded falcon.

Tian: Isis is one of the falcons that serves as the mascot for the
Air Force Academy. Lieutenant Wilson was returning with
her from Houston. The bird had her own seat. She was
much better behaved than some passengers.

Chris: Does she collect frequent flier miles?

Tian: No idea. Can you talk tonight?
Chris: Yes. In a half hour.
Tian: Ok. I'm going to shower now then.

Curled up with a cup of lemon herbal tea, Tian read an ebook while waiting for Chris's call. The couple had reached the break up point of the book after his ex-girlfriend sabotaged them. Her attention wandered from the book. She'd called Chris her boyfriend, but how could they be when they hardly saw each other? For the next six months, she wanted to spend as much of her time off as possible with her dad. They'd only made a start in repairing the relationship.

Tian closed the book app and opened her work calendar for February. As promised, her father had arranged for the flight to Paris, and she had another one to Rio to complete her necessary 787 flight hours. She'd also bid on several flights to or through Boston's Logan airport, making it easier to see her parents. There wasn't room to add in a relationship with a boyfriend.

If Chris even qualified as a boyfriend. At this point, he was a friend she'd kissed. Platinum-level amazing kisses. He qualified even if women usually saw their boyfriends more than once a week. Nothing like a long-distance relationship with the man who lived next door.

The half hour mark passed and then the hour mark.

Tian: Still waiting for your call. Half an hour until I need to go to bed.

The phone rang.

"Hey, sorry. I was waiting for you to call."

Tian put her phone on speaker and reviewed their texts. "Oh, we didn't say who was going to call."

Chris laughed. "I wasted an hour watching hockey when I could have been talking to you."

An hour she'd spent realizing that they were fooling themselves to think a relationship would work. She wouldn't break up over the phone, though. Been there, done that, both as recipient and deliverer.

"I was reading a mediocre romance."

"No happily ever after?"

"I'm sure it will have one. They always do." She needed to change the subject. "You should have seen the falcon. She was gorgeous."

"Birds flying on a plane. Reminds me of that t-shirt you wore when we first met."

Oh no, he was getting sentimental after only two and a half weeks of knowing each other.

"I hadn't thought about that. Besides the Air Force, a couple of bird sanctuaries may fly with their birds of prey, including bald eagles on commercial airlines. Although the eagle has a special cage."

"It seems like the Air Force would fly them on their own planes."

"I assume they do." Tian ran out of things to say about the bird. She'd only seen her for a moment, as the bird was first on board.

"Anything else interesting happen today?" asked Chris.

"Not really. I flew with Cook again. I like his style, and he doesn't hit on me or talk down to me, which is a bonus."

"Do you expect every man to be a jerk to you?"

His question caused her to pause. "I hope they won't be, but I am usually on my guard."

"That is a sad way to live."

"How else should I?"

"I don't know. You are talking to someone who is paid to see threats everywhere and hope he is wrong."

"Wow. Neither of us looks for the good. Kind of depressing." Tian yawned.

"That's the most depressing thing we could have in common."

Tian tried to laugh. It sounded like a sick seal.

"You sound tired." His voice was as soothing as a cup of hot chocolate.

"I should go to bed. I have a 9:00 a.m. flight to LAX."

"Call tomorrow?"

"Sure. Only next time, let's decide who is calling whom."

"Agreed, sleep well. I'd say don't let the bedbugs bite, but I am sure you already checked. Be safe."

"Yes, I did. Night, Chris."

Tian checked her alarm and connected the charger. The conversation had been like her book—less than satisfying. She wouldn't feel as bad about ending the relationship after another two nights of generic conversation.

Green rooms were rarely green. The depth of Chris's thoughts reached a new low as he waited in the room next to the sound stage where Candace gave her second interview of the day promoting her theme park for critically and terminally ill children and their families ahead of the national fundraising campaign with the goal to purchase two planes to shuttle children for whom a standard commercial flight presented too many dangers. Having heard the presentation several times, Chris could answer questions as well as the Ogilvie's PR firm.

A man entered the room. Chris brought his thoughts back to the present as he analyzed the newcomer with the familiar face.

The make-up artist rushed in. "Mr. Kirkpatrick, if you would come with me. Those lights will wash out your face."

That is where he'd seen the man—political ads. He was running for senator. Chris relaxed. He may not agree with the man's politics, but he was not likely to threaten the Ogilvies either.

The sound of clapping penetrated the door to the studio. The interview was over. He only had to wait a few moments for Candace to enter the room. Chris stayed back as a tech removed the microphone.

Dana came through another door and stopped next to Candace.

"The audience loved you."

"If they will only donate. We have enough for one plane, but there are personnel to pay, maintenance, crew, pilots..." Candace adjusted her jacket. "I have an interview in the conference room on the fourth floor. I need to stop at a restroom on the way up."

"There is one on the other side of hair and make-up," offered Dana.

The last interview finished at two. Chris held the SUV door open for Candace.

"Next stop—home. I have no desire to speak to anyone but family for the rest of the day."

Chris climbed into the passenger seat. Dana entered another vehicle headed for the school. The driver dropped them at the front door of Two Garden Tower. Chris followed Candace into the elevator.

"You've been quiet today. What is up?"

"Nothing."

Candace studied him. "I am not overly convinced of that. Do you have plans for tonight, since I won't need you?"

"No." It was a mistake to call the billionaire's wife by her first name. Now she thought she could comment on his personal life.

"What about the pilot?"

"She's working today and tomorrow."

"That must make it hard to get to know her."

"Our schedules are not exactly complimentary."

They reached the penthouse. Candace pushed the hold button, keeping the elevator open. "If I can do anything to help, let me know."

"Why?"

"Because you have been with me off and on for the last two years, and I have never seen you so—I'm not sure of the word...smitten? —as I did in Spokane when you arranged things for Tian. Everyone deserves a chance at a relationship. It would be a shame if you didn't get one. Maybe you can do something for Valentine's Day."

"She'll be in Paris." The most romantic place in the world on the day of romance. The irony that it would be a long-distance holiday for them stung.

"Work?"

"Yes."

"Well, that doesn't help, does it?" Candace released the hold button and stepped out of the elevator.

Chris tapped his on-call status into the Hastings's app.

A text from the dispatcher popped up: Go to C&O and relieve Ben, please.

Chris: Crawford?

Dispatch: Yes.

So much for a quiet afternoon.

Fifteen

With last night's conversation in mind, Tian entered the pilot's lounge at LAX. All conversation stopped. At midday, she expected a few more pilots to be in the room. Instead, five from different airlines looked up from the table where they sat.

Just her luck, one was the pilot from the airline she'd vowed to avoid. If Chris were there, she would show him exhibit "A" for why she kept her defenses up all the time. The man sneered at her. Tian took a seat at the farthest computer and pulled up the weather information for her next destination.

Dad had mentioned switching airlines. Glancing at the pilots around the table, she eliminated two airlines from her list. Every pilot she'd met from either of the airlines had been rude and full of themselves. The handful of female pilots she'd met from those airlines looked down on everyone. She'd heard the benefits weren't as good as Legacy Air's either. Her fingers hovered over the keys, a job search only a stroke away, but no telling who might walk in and see over her shoulder.

Captain Rochester complained off and on during their flight from Chicago. After redoing her hair, he should have beat her to the lounge. If he didn't come in soon she'd need to send someone to find him.

She finished her prep work, but still no other Legacy pilots entered the lounge. Tian was about to call Rochester when whispers at the table alerted her to a change in the room. Not wanting to draw any attention to herself, Tian waited before looking up. Not one, but two female pilots had entered the lounge.

Four bars on the older woman's epaulets indicated her status as a captain. She glared at the men. "Gentlemen, the FO you are ogling is my daughter. Get your minds out of the 70s."

Two of the men looked somewhat penitent.

The women joined Tian at the computer banks.

"Have they been like that for long?" asked the captain.

"Since I got here."

"I've been flying for over thirty years. Every time I think we've made progress, I run into a group like that. I'm Marta; this is my daughter Megan. We rarely fly together, but our airline wanted some female publicity. You know the drill. I liked the article on Legacy last fall. Good job."

"I see my photographs precede me. I go by Tian, by the way."

"That and the videos," said Megan.

"I'm afraid they gave me more attention than I wanted."

Marta sat at the computer next to Tian. "Get used to it. Every four years or so, someone gets it in their mind to feature female pilots in an effort to recruit. Doesn't do much good. I have to congratulate Legacy though. They're the first airline to make truly significant changes to their benefits to attract females. I wish I'd had maternity leave and work options like you have."

"I'm hoping to transfer to Legacy if our carrier doesn't change things." Megan turned the ring on her left hand around to show a small round cut diamond. "We want a family, but it is so hard with this job."

Tian nodded her agreement and removed a third major carrier from her list, leaving cargo and corporate as options.

"Back in the day, I had to take a step down and fly short domestic routes so I could be home most nights. And I've been a victim of Aviation Induced Divorce Syndrome, twice. You've got it good at

Legacy. We may tease about the nepotism, but what your aunt did for women flyers is the best thing since Amelia Earhart."

Tian kept her voice low. "Are you saying that you wished you worked for Legacy?"

Marta nodded. "I'm interested in the part-time options I'm hearing rumors about."

"You are hearing things I don't know about." Tian heard a rumor, of course, but nothing to share, especially with a pilot she'd just met. Tian stood and glanced at the clocks on the wall, one on local time and the other on Zulu. "If you'll excuse me, I should meet the captain for my next flight."

During their conversation, several more pilots had entered the room. Among them were Captain Cook and Tim. Tim glanced at her then took the terminal farthest away.

Cook crossed the room to her. "Please tell me you are my FO back to Dallas."

"That isn't how it works, and you know it. I am on a flight to Seattle. I was looking for Rochester."

"He'll be here in a moment. I saw him in the washroom." Cook maneuvered her to a corner. "Can't you trade?"

"What is wrong?"

"He didn't stop talking the entire flight." Cook inclined his head to indicate Tim.

"You know I can't do that, but it is nice to be wanted."

Cook rolled his eyes. "Your captain just came in. You'd better go. I think he was running late."

Tian crossed the room to the winded pilot.

Rochester placed his hands on the back of a chair. "There you are. I'm not feeling well. I've put in for a relief pilot. Go meet the crew and brief them."

She'd only taken a few steps away when a commotion behind her caused her to look back. Rochester was lying on the floor. She reached for the airport phone on the wall and dialed 0. "We need medical to the pilot's lounge. Captain Rochester of Legacy

Air just collapsed." The operator took the few details she knew. Seeing that the captain was attended to, Tian went in search of the cabin crew huddled around a table in the next room. Chaz seemed to be the leader of the team.

"Hey, Chaz and everyone. I come with some not-so-good news. Rochester collapsed. He came in to tell me he called for a relief pilot. And then…" Tian struggled with her emotions. Part of her wanted to stay and figure out what was going on, but she knew that they needed to get the flight going.

"Should I worry? This is the second flight to Seattle I've been on with you this month, and the other one didn't go well either," said Chaz.

Tian held up her hands. "Not my fault. Let's be as ready as we can. A relief pilot should be here soon."

Chaz pulled out a chair and Tian joined them.

Five minutes later, Captain Cook came over. "Rochester is awake. They are taking him to the hospital."

"Thanks for coming to let us know."

"That isn't the only reason I'm here. Looks like they are playing a game of musical chairs. I'm now flying Seattle since it leaves first and I have the right hours. The relief is driving into the airport, he will take my DFW flight."

Chaz filled the captain in on crew concerns. Tian talked about the weather as they hurried to their gate and an on-time departure.

Tian waited until they were at cruising altitude to ask the question that plagued the back of her mind. "So, did you volunteer for this game of musical cockpits?"

"Pretty much. I don't have the patience to deal with a chatty FO for the rest of the day."

"So, you want me to be quiet?"

"No. I want something of substance to the conversation, not a rundown of every button we have at our fingertips."

"I promise not to ask you the purpose of any button, knob, or dial in the cockpit." Tian paused for a moment, then pointed at a spot near his window. "Oh, except for that purple one. I've never seen that before."

Cook glanced to his side as Tian laughed.

The captain shook his head.

"Is he that bad, or are you a bit of a grump today?"

"Probably a bit of a grump. There was an accident in my old squadron yesterday. I didn't know the airman that passed, but I still mourn with them."

"I'm sorry."

"Thanks."

They turned the conversation to other topics for the remainder of the routine flight. He was a good guy. If she were to be in a relationship with a pilot again, she'd choose Cook, only she wasn't attracted to him. Chris still filled that space, and she couldn't wait to get to the hotel for her nightly call to him. What was she thinking? She was supposed to end things. A little longer wouldn't hurt that much more would it?

Chris waited at the curb searching for Tian's hat, hoping she would appear before he was told to move on. The reflective yellow jacket of a security officer appeared in his rearview mirror at the same moment that Tian emerged from the crowd of passengers. Under the watchful eye of airport security, Tian put her bags in the back seat and climbed into the front.

"I would have gotten out and assisted you, but that man looked serious about the drivers-don't-leave-your-cars thing." He handed her a thermos of hot chocolate.

"Not complaining. You're spoiling me." Tian leaned back against the headrest. "So much nicer than the blue line."

Chris checked over his shoulder before merging into traffic. "Glad my SUV tops plastic seats on the L. Be warned—I can't guarantee this service every time you return."

"Sometimes I can catch a ride with Simone or Brit to the airport. My schedule rarely works for rides on my return."

"I noticed you don't have a parking space."

"Checking up on me?"

"Maybe a little." He smiled and glanced her direction. His safety-first mantra kept him from holding her hand while driving.

"We share the two cars, depending on the schedule. I pay my portion of the insurance and maintenance. Brit drives the most, although in the winter, she is just as likely to take the blue line since it is faster than rush hour traffic."

"Would you like a ride to the last self-defense class tomorrow?"

"Is it the end of the month already?"

Chris chuckled as he merged with freeway traffic. "You sound like me. I can't decide if January flew by or if it was slower than normal."

"February is going to be weird too. I don't have a flight until Sunday, which is to São Paulo—"

"As in Brazil?"

"Yup, then Paris on the thirteenth with my father, which will complete my training hours. Then I'll be on domestic flights until I get more flight hours. Simone put me on as many flights in and out of Boston as she could."

"That was nice of her."

"I'll miss her being in scheduling when she rejoins the cabin crew, although Brit is putting in for a transfer."

"You have almost a full week off?" Oh, the plans they could make—as long as his schedule wasn't impacted by more of his co-workers colds.

"Only five days."

"Do you have time for a date in those days?"

A too-long pause answered his question. What could she be weighing? Was she seeing the same logistical issues with their relationship he did? Was she going to back out before they even began?

"I was thinking of going to Boston on Thursday and Friday. If your schedule allows, we can squeeze something in before that." Her voice was too measured, too cautious.

"Today is my day off. And I should be off after class on Tuesday and Wednesday night."

"Then it sounds like we have some date time."

"That reminds me. Abbie Harmon left me a message. She said she couldn't reach you. She and her mom have decided to teach you a personal advanced class. They just need to know when to schedule."

"How did I earn a personal class with them?"

"Once Melanie realized you were a pilot, she thought that learning some moves for cramped quarters might be helpful. She has taken a particular interest in you."

"Is that weird?"

"From what ZoElle says, no. Melanie excels in planning and loves a challenge."

"I've had a couple of blocked number calls. And some Chicago area numbers I didn't recognize. Could one of those be hers?"

Chris took the exit for Two Garden Tower. "I'll text you Melanie's number."

"What else do you have planned for today?"

"Laundry and a workout. Every single piece of equipment at last night's hotel was damaged."

"I was planning a swim this afternoon. Do you want to join me?"

"Mmm. If I join you, I can't watch you from the treadmill."

Did you like what you saw? Instead of asking the first question that popped into his mind, Chris searched for something else to say. "You could always water walk."

Like the notes of a music box, Tian's laughter filled the car. "Then you'll know I'm watching you."

"I'd know, anyway." He waited for the gate to rise for the underground garage.

"Fine. I'll meet you in the pool in one hour."

Sixteen

SHE MUST BE CRAZY. AFTER her night in Denver and the conversation with Marta and Megan, Tian had intended to end their relationship with Chris before they grew closer. No sense causing them both more pain. Instead, she was counting laps in the pool in the lane next to Chris. He kept with her slow pace as well as a synchronized swimmer.

At the end of the lap, Tian held on to the edge of the pool, unable to touch in the six-foot end. "Go at your own pace. It isn't like we can talk or anything."

Chris dove under the divider. He came up mere inches from her and shook his head like a dog, spritzing her with water. Tian used her arm to splash him back. He dove again, lifting her by the waist and tossing her down the lane. Fight or flight? Tian chose flight and took off. Chris caught up with her a few strokes later, grabbing her ankle and pulling her back. Tian made the mistake of opening her mouth and instead of saying his name, she sucked in water.

"Aggg." She twisted around to splash him. He grasped her wrist and pulled her to him.

They'd moved enough towards the middle of the pool that he was standing. Tian strained her toes to touch. She steadied herself with a hand on his shoulder.

"It seems to me there is quite a bit we can do if I keep pace with you."

"Like what? Splash me?"

He wrapped an arm around her waist, fitting her against him, and lunged back, bringing them further into the pool.

"What are you doing?"

"I'm catching a mermaid."

"You're the better swimmer in this scenario. Are you sure you aren't a merman?"

"Hmm, I'll drag you down to my lair and keep you as my queen."

She brought her other hand to his shoulder, aware of every place they touched. He was all muscle and warmth. With his wet hair slicked back, he looked like a model for any number of fantasy paintings of a merman. "And what would you do then?"

His face moved closer to hers. "Forget about all the craziness of the land lovers and live happily under the sea."

"That sounds very nice. I wonder if I'd like swimming all day instead of flying?" Her voice came out husky.

"Hold your breath." It was all the warning he gave her before they submerged.

His kiss was not unexpected, though it felt weird as the water pulled at her, trying to separate them. Desperately, she maintained the kiss. There was something sensual about fighting the pull of nature to cling to Chris. She adjusted her hands so one was behind his head and the other at the base of his neck, afraid if the kiss were to end, she would gasp and drown. Not likely; Chris would protect her.

He tightened his arms around her and brought them both to the surface. Now that the water no longer tried to separate them, his lips moved over hers without the fear of separation. Tian wrapped a leg around his to hold herself steady.

She'd never kissed in a pool before. This was the kiss that should have been on her bucket list that she didn't know about. Anything higher than triple platinum?

Chris ended the kiss and rested his forehead against hers, his hands still framing her face. They both drew ragged breaths.

Above their heads, a speaker crackled. "Congratulations. You were underwater long enough to set off the electronic lifeguard. Considering the way you were giving mouth to mouth, we will not be sending security."

Chris glared at the security camera. "Javier!"

Laughter boomed over the speaker.

Another voice spoke, "The judges are giving you a 4.8 for synchronized swimming. It would have been lower, but they are impressed—" With a pop the speaker switched off.

Tian released her hold on Chris. "I forget they are always watching. Is there really an electronic lifeguard?"

"First time I've heard of it. But Colin Ogilvie is always inventing things… No telling what he might be testing."

She rolled her eyes. "That was an embarrassing end to a kiss."

Chris took her hand and tugged her into swimming to the side of the pool. "I thought kissing underwater would be different. I guess I am not meant to be a merman after all."

"It was fun to try. Even if we had your roommate and who-knows-all watching?" Tian turned to the camera and made a face. "Way to ruin a workout, Javier!"

"I doubt he's listening. I'm not sure this room is mic'd."

"Next time I see him, I'll make sure he's listening. I have a few choice words for him. I am not fond of voyeurs."

Chris pulled himself out of the pool and sat on the edge. He'd make an impressive merman. "Done?"

Tian swam to the ladder to climb out. "I'd better go finish that laundry. And schedule my class with Hastings."

A mother and three children entered through the locker rooms. It took a moment for Tian to recognize Candace Ogilvie.

Dana carried an assortment of pool noodles. "Leaving?"

Tian wrapped her beach towel around her, tucking in the end to leave her hands free. "Yes, the pool is all yours."

The oldest boy stopped to high five Chris before jumping into the pool. Dana followed.

Candace set a pile of towels on the bench next to Tian's bag. "Have you met our children? The tall one is Porter. He is seven. Pollyanna is five, and Peter is three. I never thought I would be a mother, let alone have three children at once."

"I haven't met them." She'd heard Candace discuss them in vague terms on her podcast. An acquaintance who'd lost her battle with cancer had asked Candace to take them when she died. On the Podcast, she referred to them as Hewey, Dewey, and Lewey to protect their identities.

Candace whistled. All three children stopped playing. "Kids, say hi to Miss Johnson. She's a pilot."

"You fly planes?"

"Are they big?"

"Did you fly the one Mom was on?" the children talked over each other.

"Yes, to all three questions."

Pollyanna tilted her head. "I thought pilots were boys."

"Not all of them."

"Can I fly with you someday?" asked Peter.

Tian looked at Candace and waited for a subtle nod before answering. "I think that can be arranged."

"Yo! I get to fly an airplane!" Peter immediately splashed his sister.

Pollyanna ducked and sent him a frown. "I can fly too, can't I, Mom?"

"You will all fly on an airplane, but the pilot will be flying it." At Candace's clarification, the boys lost interest in the conversation and swam off.

"Will you fly Mom's new plane? It's for sick kids."

"I fly for Legacy Air."

"Oh." Her face fell, and she swam off too.

"The children have been very excited about getting planes to transport terminally ill children and their families to Robyn's Place. It's a theme park for seriously ill children."

"That sounds exciting." Tian had heard about the monumental project on a podcast.

"If you ever want to jump ship—or plane—let me know. I'm on the hunt for pilots who want to do something a bit out of the ordinary. The ride itself will be part of the adventure for these children, so the pilots need to be open to lots of questions and some on-the-ground flying lessons. The cabin crew are pediatric nurses in disguise. I'm hoping to have everything in place by June when the planes should be ready. Camouflaging medical equipment takes time."

"I assume there would be no seat-commandeering passengers with their pets onboard."

"Thor is not invited. We may fly some service dogs. Well-behaved, of course. And all the seats are first class."

"No irate passengers? Pilots must be lining up for this job." An amazing opportunity for someone. The competition would be fierce.

"I hope so. I'll let you two go." Candace looked over Tian's shoulder to Chris and waved goodbye.

Tian turned. "I didn't know you were there."

"I wanted to see if you had dinner plans." He held open the door to the hallway.

Tian pushed the elevator button. "My place?"

"Sounds good to me. What time?"

"About an hour?"

"That should give me enough time to beat up my roommate." Chris's smile indicated that Javier wasn't in any real trouble.

"Hit him once for me."

They separated at the elevator. Thoughts swirled in Tian's head. Most were about Chris and the kiss. How could she end a relationship she wanted so badly?

"Jerk move with the intercom." Chris chucked his damp towel at Javier's head.

"It was either that or have the Ogilvies walk in on you. I don't think they'd appreciate you giving the kids an up-close and personal human relations lesson."

"We were only kissing."

"Um-hmm." Javier threw the towel back.

Chris caught it easily. "Is there a drowning monitor?"

"No, but there should be. When I first looked at the pool to see if it was empty, I didn't notice you underwater. I gave Dana the all clear, and then you surfaced."

"There are other things you could have said to get us to leave the pool. Tian is paranoid that the building is watching her."

"It is. At least in all the public areas." Javier's acknowledgement wasn't anything Chris wasn't aware of before. Then it hadn't inconvenienced him before, either.

"I told her I'd beat you up."

"Ha. Like you could."

"Sparring. Anytime. Hastings."

"Tomorrow morning at 5:00 a.m.?"

Chris's phone pinged.

> **Tian: Abbie is sending a car for me. Says she wants to do an advanced defense session tonight. Late dinner?**

He stared at the phone for a long moment. If Abbie was sending a car, she must be doing the personal class at her estate. He'd heard stories about the gym Abbie and her husband had set up.

> **Chris: Sure.**

He pocketed his phone and turned back to Javier. "5:00 a.m. works."

Javier raised a brow. "Who killed your puppy?"

"What?"

"The text. What's up?" asked Javier.

"Tian is having a private self-defense lesson with Abbie tonight."

"As in Abbie Hastings Harmon?" Javier flipped his fingers, making a clicking sound Chris could never master.

"At her estate."

"Wow, are these your apology sessions?"

"Yup." Chris set his phone on the charging pad.

"You better hope there are not too many of them, or she'll end up being able to take you down."

"Correction. You better hope there are not too many of them. She was less than thrilled about the pool commentary you made."

Over the next three hours, Chris completed any number of chores, including cleaning his bathroom and mopping the kitchen.

Finally, Tian's text rescued him.

Tian: Home. Are you still hungry?

Chris: Yes.

Tian: Come on over.

She didn't need to ask twice. Chris bolted from his room and down the hall, barely maintaining a walk.

Tian answered his knock. "That was quick. You must be starved."

"Not quite. I had one of Javier's empanadas."

"I am, so I'm breaking out the frozen meals. Italian or Hawaiian chicken?"

"Both?" His comment had the desired outcome, and he was blessed with one of Tian's laughs.

"Okay then, two double-size dinners."

"Two?"

"Abbie gave me a major workout. You should see the homework I have. I'm going to have to double my workout time." She rubbed her shoulder. "And invest in some flexible ice packs."

"I have some. If you like, I can grab a couple while you're heating dinner."

"I might just have to kiss you for that."

Chris bent and brushed his lips against hers. "Payment accepted."

"I never took you as a mercenary." She wrapped her arms around his neck and gave him a kiss worth more than a bag of ice.

"I didn't take you for..." Chris couldn't come up with something to say that didn't border on trashy.

Tian pulled back and tapped his chin. "Good, because I'm not. It was an excuse to finish what was so rudely interrupted this afternoon. However, I *am* hungry. So if you'll go get the ice pack, your dinner will be waiting."

Chris hurried to his apartment. This relationship could not be kept waiting.

Seventeen

The days moved faster than Tian expected. Brazil or not, it was the first time she could remember wishing that she was somewhere other than a cockpit. By now, she'd hoped to find a reason other than their jobs her relationship with Chris wouldn't work. Instead, she found reason after reason to make it work. They laughed over games on his gaming system. He should have never challenged her to *Fightsym IV: Zombies in the Air*. Then there were the hours he spent in the gym helping her through Abbie's strenuous workout. The only reason she had to end the relationship was work.

Lame.

Double lame.

Tian aimed her flashlight into the landing gear to dispel the shadows created by the airport's bright lights. The chill seeped in where her gloves met her coat as she completed her assigned exterior preflight checks and returned to the plane for their evening flight. She shed her coat and hung it in a closet near the outside of the cockpit. The pilots spoke on the other side of the open cockpit door.

"She may be his daughter, but she's as cold as ice."

"I don't believe it."

"I'm telling you, don't try. She'll shut you down."

"That's what you said about the redheaded flight attendant." The man laughed. The sound sent a chill up Tian's spine. The uncomfortable feeling that she was eavesdropping on a conversation about her grew.

Taking a deep breath, she entered the cockpit and handed the checklist to the captain. "Nothing unusual. I can see a film of ice. I assume we are going through the deicer."

"Ground is recommending it for all planes tonight," said Captain Andrew Parish. His voice was the one of warning in the earlier conversation. Good. Tian would rather not have to fend off advances from the person in charge. Although this was her first flight with Captain Parish, she knew his reputation. He didn't drink, never had coffee, and was a dedicated family man—something to do with his religion. He even attended church on Sunday when his schedule permitted. Would he attend in Brazil? Did he speak Portuguese? Probably, if he did this flight often.

The rest of the pre-flight and take off were routine. Two hours into the flight, the other officer left his seat. "First rest rotation?"

The captain nodded. "I'll take second. Tian, you get third."

The overnight flight was already playing with Tian's body clock. She didn't relish being last for the break, but perhaps it was for the best. She would be alert for the landing.

When the officer left, Tian moved up into his seat.

"I knew your mother back in the day."

"Really?" She knew several of the older pilots must, but they never mentioned her. Probably since they worked with her dad.

"I heard she became a nurse. She'd be a good one."

"Mom loves being an RN."

"I warned her about your father. Well, I hope you listen better than she did. Stay away from Ludmiller. He pilots a decent flight, but he's ten times worse than your father ever was. He's set his sights on you. Don't be alone with him outside of the cockpit."

"Thanks for the heads up. I don't intend to socialize with him."

"Good for you. Stay away from anyone in the industry, I say. I've been married for thirty-two years now. It hasn't been easy on either of us, but I take my vows seriously, and my wife knows it. All this new technology helps. I can message her from every place I go, and she can message me. I used to write her and the kids letters every night. Most of the time now I can FaceTime her."

"They featured the two of you in the Centennial piece, didn't they?"

"Yup, I'm one of the Pitt descendants. My piece wasn't as big as yours. None of my kids want to follow me into the industry." Andrew laughed good naturedly.

"I think you had more words. I got more photos. Anything to recruit more women."

"It's a hard life. Easier now that I only take long-haul flights. I try to see something new on every trip and add something to my postcard collection."

The time flew by as it always did, all puns intended and true. Soon it was captain's turn for a rest period. True to his promise, the other FO tried every bit of flattery in the book. Mild rebuffs didn't work on him.

Tian gave up in disgust. "I have a boyfriend I am committed to." Not a lie. "I have no intention of getting involved with you or another Legacy employee." *Been there, done that.* "So how about we stick to our favorite sports teams or movie trivia and doing our jobs? Don't delude yourself that I am playing some game. Either accept that nothing is happening between us, or I take this to HR."

He looked like someone had slapped him. "You're kidding, right?"

"No." Tian kept eye contact with him.

"Don't report me."

"I won't, as long as you keep things professional. Got it?"

"How about those Bulls? Do you think they have a chance this season?"

Tian turned back to the window in front of her. "I don't know. The Cavaliers are looking pretty good."

"Cleveland?" Ludmiller behaved for the rest of the flight.

Once again, the cabin crew ended up in a different hotel. Since Tian's knowledge of Portuguese was limited to a few phrases, she had no choice but to explore São Paulo alone with the aid of her map app and the subway. She sent most of the photos she took to Chris.

The first night, they managed long conversations on the phone. The second day, while visiting an art museum, Tian received a text bringing her back to the reality of their jobs.

> Chris: The family is going to Seattle for the week. I am part of the detail. I won't be back until you are gone again. I'll text when I can.
>
> Tian: Be safe.

How many times had they said 'be safe' to each other? There wasn't anything else to say. Saying more would be to admit she felt more.

If he was correct about the schedule, they would go at least two weeks without seeing each other. Maybe their jobs were as big of an obstacle as she'd thought.

The masterpieces and art exhibits lost their allure. Instead of seeing beauty in them, she found they reflected her mood. The knife in a still life? Threatened an end. The river in a landscape? Swept away dreams. The women watching boats on the horizon? Just said goodbye to a lover who would die in a shipwreck, never to return. She tried to tell herself it was only two weeks.

Tian returned to the hotel minutes before sunset. She entered the elevator and was followed by a man about her age. He pushed the button for the floor above hers. Keeping her distance, Tian leaned against the wall opposite him. The man pushed another button, stopping the elevator. He stepped closer. The overabundance of cheap aftershave he wore turned her stomach. How many times had she been told to pay attention to her surroundings?

The man leered at her.

He spoke words not in her limited vocabulary, but his meaning was clear.

"No." Tian glared and pointed to the elevator bank.

He reached for her. Tian grabbed his wrist as she'd practiced. The man was smaller than Chris and easier to propel away as she switched to the side of the elevator with the controls.

"I said no." She kept her voice firm and pushed the button for the lobby. The elevator responded by going up. Tian stepped off at her floor but stood by the door staring him down. He didn't exit. As soon as the door closed, Tian closed her eyes and took a deep breath. She opened them and, seeing she was alone, gave a fist pump before walking to her room. As soon as she was inside, she bolted the door.

Having him take revenge was not on her list of activities. Wow, what Abbie taught her worked. How to let Chris know without worrying him?

> **Tian: I got to use one of the moves Abbie taught me in real life.**
> **I'm perfectly safe. Thanks for the lessons and the practice.**

She probably should tell someone about the incident, but who? The English speakers at the front desk were as proficient as she was in Portuguese. She opted for Simone and made the video call.

"Wow, Brazil must be boring if you are calling me."

"Not exactly. Is there a number we're supposed to call if there is an incident?"

"What do you mean?"

"A man entered the elevator after me. He did something to make it stop. He came toward me, calling me Chica, and reached for me. I put the self-defense lesson to good use, restarted the elevator, and got out. He didn't follow me."

Simone shuddered. "Where are the rest of the crew?"

"I don't know. Only the pilots are at this hotel, and I'm avoiding one of them."

"Oh, anyone for your 'don't fly' list?"

"No, I think we have an understanding."

"Here's the number." Simone added the number to a chat box. "Just tell them what you told me. They'll let you know if you need to do anything else. See you tomorrow."

"Day after. It is another all-night flight." Tian ended the call.

The person who answered the hotline was nice, although they asked a multitude of questions. No, she didn't remember his shoes. In the end, she was told to stay close to others—advice she could have given herself. Since there wasn't anyone for her to pal around with, she stayed in her hotel room for the rest of the night.

Which, of course, only gave her too much time to think. Chris was foremost in her mind.

Chris read the text again. It bothered him that he wasn't in a position to call. It could have been worse. Tian could have texted the words "don't worry" which always had the exact opposite effect. However, since she texted that the classes had been successful, he needed to trust that she'd gotten away from the danger.

Chris: I have a hundred questions. I trust you are safe.

Tian: Yes, I am. A bit freaked out is all. I don't have anyone to hang out with since the crew is in another hotel. If I am to ever do long haul flights on a regular basis I am going to ask to be in their hotel.

Chris: Why aren't you in the same hotel?

Tian: No idea. It must have to do with what our unions negotiated. Or our late checkout tomorrow.

Dana came out of the hotel suite. "Family is settled in. The kids want to go swimming, of course. Did you check out the pool?"

"Pretty standard for a hotel."

"The parents aren't going down. So I'll need a second since I'm in the water. Ben says you win. I'll take hall duty while you change into something less formal than a suit."

Chris: I'll text more later.

The three kids must have stored up energy on the flight. They made instant friends with the other hotel visitors in the pool and played a rousing round of Marco Polo. A mother kept glancing his way. She wasn't checking him out the same way her teenage daughter had. The jeans and polo he changed into drew attention in the swimming area.

Finally, the woman wrapped a hotel robe around her and came over to where he sat. "I think you should leave," she said.

"Sorry, I can't." Chris scanned the room over the woman's shoulder.

"What type of a pervert are you watching kids swim? I saw you look at my daughter. She's underage, you know."

Chris ignored the woman hoping she'd realize the obvious and back away.

"Look at me when I talk to you." Her voice raised.

Chris crossed his arms. "Ma'am, will you please move to the side?"

"I'm not going to move. You should move."

"I am currently acting as a lifeguard. Please do not stand between me and my children."

"You are overdressed and the sign says 'No Lifeguard on Duty.'"

Chris sidestepped to open a path between him and the children.

"I'm going to report you."

"Yes, ma'am."

"You want me to, so I'll leave and you can ogle my daughter." She waved her arms in front of his face.

Chris sidestepped again. "Ma'am, I asked you politely to not stand between me and the children. Please do not —"

"I can stand any place I want to. And I am going to stand in front of you to keep you away from those children."

"I wouldn't advise that." When he returned to Chicago, he needed to ask ZoElle about making a self-defense against Karens class. He had no idea what to tell the woman. He pointed to the Hastings Security logo on his shirt. "I am working at the moment. For everyone's safety, I ask that you please leave me alone."

The woman narrowed her eyes. "Nice disguise. I am reporting you."

Dana got out of the pool holding Peter's hand. She pointed to the bathroom.

"If you will excuse me." Chris walked around her and over to Peter. He escorted him to the shared family bathroom and stood outside the door. The woman kept an eye on both of them as she used the wall phone to make a call.

A moment later, the hotel manager hurried into the pool area— the same manager Chris had met with a couple of hours earlier when they'd gone over the hotel's security while the Ogilvies were at dinner. While the woman ranted and pointed, Peter exited the bathroom.

"Did you wash your hands?" Chris asked.

"But I'm going in the water."

"Wash."

Peter disappeared only long enough to run water over his hands. When he returned, the lady, still ranting, and the manger had moved their conversation closer to Chris.

"This man could be dangerous."

Peter put his hands on his hips. "He is dangerous. He's my bodyguard. He keeps bad people away. Are you bad people?"

The woman stood fish-faced for a moment before she sputtered her answer. "No. I am not."

"Then leave him alone so we can stay and play." Peter ran off to Dana's beckoning arms.

The woman's eyes narrowed. "Are you really that kid's body-guard?"

"Personal security, ma'am."

"Well, I —" She turned to the hotel manager and then back to Chris before stomping off the best one can in flip-flops and a hotel robe.

The manager apologized and left. Chris resumed his post until Dana decided it was time for the kids to return to their room.

In the elevator, Dana whispered, "Next time wear a swimming suit. She'll be too busy staring at your six pack to wonder why you aren't swimming."

Pollyanna tugged on Dana's towel. "There are no drinks allowed in the pool area."

Chris forced all of his face muscles not to react. He couldn't wait to tell Tian the joke, but by the time he was relieved from duty that night it was too late to call her.

Chris: Sweet dreams. Hope to catch you tomorrow.

Tian didn't miss Chris her first day back. She was too busy taking catnaps, trying to get her body over the two all-night flights and change in weather. The second day, she had an early morning self-defense class with Abbie at the estate. Abbie complimented her on her practicing and her practical use. Another former body-guard, Deidre, joined them.

Deidre demonstrated a move that would down an attacker. "Most attackers are not thinking offensively. Given your stature, they won't expect you to pull them anyplace—especially closer. After physics, surprise is your best friend."

"Don't try to use this move if someone is standing. You need to use their momentum," said Abbie, and she demonstrated on her brother Alex.

"I could stand here all day and my sister would never move me."

"True, unless I tickled him. But he'd get me back." Abbie pushed her brother's shoulder to prove he had a steady stance.

"Ready to try?" asked Deidre.

Tian appraised Alex. He was taller and broader than Chris by the slightest margins. "How will it work when he's expecting it?"

"I know I am practicing with you, and I remember how it was the first time Abbie took me down. I try to go with that, not making it too easy."

Abbie folded her arms. "After all these years Alex has come up with several counter moves; however, it's unlikely that your average assailant has learned them."

"Okay, then let's try this."

Three tries later, Alex sat on the mat. "Good job. You would've had me the second time if your left hand had been higher."

Abbie and Deidre high fived each other and Tian.

"If you ever want to switch careers, I could train you," said Abbie. "With your height and build…"

"No, thanks. I love flying." *Although there are some aspects of the job she wished she didn't have to put up with.*

Alex gathered his things. "I'll see you later. Are we practicing again?"

"I don't fly until the thirteenth, so if anyone can, my schedule is open. As long as I can fit in some simulator time."

Abbie scrolled through her phone. "I thought you were dating Chris Johnson. Don't you have plans with him?"

"He's in Seattle." Tian's answer meshed with Alex's.

Alex continued, "He should be home Saturday afternoon."

News to Tian.

"What about Friday at noon?" asked Abbie.

Everyone agreed on the time, and Alex took off.

"Do you have time for breakfast? Deidre is staying."

Tian looked from one woman to the other to decide if Abbie's invitation was genuine before answering. She wished she'd brought another shirt, but the offer seemed sincere. "Sure."

Abbie led them into what Tian could only call a breakfast room, not that she'd ever been in one. A house as large as this one had to have a formal dining room, and this was much too small.

Diedre scooped up a muffin from the basket in the center of the four-person table and added a banana and a boiled egg to her bowl. "Tell us about flying."

"I love it. I think it is literally in my blood. I'm a fourth-generation pilot. I find something magical about being able to be up higher than the birds. Earth looks so peaceful from above the clouds."

"But?" asked Abbie.

"As a woman, there are some downsides. It's a hard career to raise a family with. Legacy has implemented some great maternity leave policies and added more flexibility for nursing mothers. The odd schedule takes a toll on families." Tian chose a muffin to go with her boiled egg. "It's hard to maintain a relationship. I've known this great guy for a month now, but I don't think we've had ten days together."

"Are you going to do anything for Valentine's Day?" asked Deidre.

"I'll be in Paris."

"Wow, Paris for Valentine's Day."

"With my Dad and my sister. And I will have been up most of the night before flying. Not quite as cool as it sounds."

Deidre drank a smoothie that smelled like peanut butter. "Definitely not as fun as going with a boyfriend or husband. The kissing spots at the Eiffel Tower would be wasted."

"If I have a boyfriend that long." Tian hadn't meant to let the thought slip out.

Abbie set down her fork. "Now you have me curious. I don't know Chris well, but you looked cute together. Is it still the way you met? I was in a conversation with ZoElle and Mom regarding what happened. ZoElle was in shock that he did that. It is so not like him."

"Did what?" asked Deidre.

Tian related the story of how they'd met. "I think he reacted to me yelling and leaping across the room. He wasn't angry. Like almost zero emotion."

"I'm married to a bodyguard. My husband and I have both learned not to sneak up on each other. One hundred percent not wise. I may or may not have given him a black eye on our honeymoon." Deidre smiled, but Abbie's laughter confirmed that the husband had suffered an unintended punch from his bride.

"It's more our schedules. We both love what we do, but it is like having a long-distance relationship. We can't move forward. I need to be attracted to an accountant or someone who has a nice, boring job." Tian finished her breakfast.

"If only love were that easy," said Abbie.

"I don't know how I would change my job. I've come to the conclusion that I work for the best airline, and I don't want to go back to flying regional so I can be close to home base all the time. Not to mention the pay cut. And I'm not going to ask Chris to change his career. He loves what he does."

"That is a tough position. I gave up my job when we married. It wasn't practical to be a bodyguard when my new life required me to have one. I spent a few months improving my photography skills. There are also plenty of charities to be involved in. Now I have the boys. I am more than busy enough."

"You also keep up with things at Hastings, don't you?"

"More now that the boys are in school part of the day. It is hard not to when my family is so involved." Abbie folded her napkin and set it on the table.

"I didn't have to change careers, but after our daughter was born, I wanted to step away from the action into a cushy desk job. Since my father-in-law owns the security group my husband worked for, it was an easy enough move."

"I want motherhood, eventually. I didn't think of how it worked with a career at eighteen."

Abbie leaned forward. "My mother said that's one of the beauties of being a woman. We can rebuild ourselves and our careers many times. Right now, she claims to be working on her grandma degree, but I know she still plans out some of Hastings's protocols."

"I never thought of that." Tian filed the thought away to examine when she was alone.

Deidre stood. "Speaking of jobs and children, I need to attend to both. Thank you for breakfast. I'll see you both on Friday."

Abbie called for a car, and Tian enjoyed a quiet ride home. The thoughts expressed by her friends didn't solve her immediate problem. How could she date someone long enough to make long-term plans? She didn't know any accountants.

Eighteen

Chris folded the last of his Hastings Security polos back into his suitcase. The week had gone better than expected. The bodyguards from the Seattle group were topnotch and provided hotel coverage, meaning the Hastings team were able to sleep and focus on the excursions. Best of all, Candace completed her business with the airplane conversion team early, and Colin finished his negotiations with the software firm in record time. The children were treated to a number of excursions, and everyone could return to Chicago a day ahead of schedule. Which meant he could see Tian.

Sharing a hotel room wasn't conducive to communication—meaning text messages and not-so-private phone calls were short and sweet. Too short and not enough sweet. He knew they would have more to talk about if he wasn't so concerned with listening ears. Last night's phone call left him with the irritating feeling that Tian wanted to say more, but he was prevented from pressing the issue when he knew others could hear him. He wanted to say more for that matter. Talking to her was more relaxing than his mixed music.

He checked the hotel room for anything he may have forgotten and set his bag on the cart with the rest of the team's stuff to take down to the SUVs. The family's bags waited on a second cart. Chris joined the family in their suite.

Candace sat on the end of the couch with a tearful Pollyanna next to her. Taking a position near the door, he stood with a passive expression, presumably ignoring the mother/daughter conversation unfolding in front of him. Chris heard enough of the conversation to understand that Pollyanna didn't want to go home. Dana emerged from one of the bedrooms with a robot toy followed by the boys.

"We wanted to leave it to see if it would find its way home like in the movie…" Porter's tone had taken on a tired sort of whine. Candace and Colin had chosen to return at night in hopes of the children sleeping on the plane. Seeing the children near meltdown phase, Chris hoped they were right.

The Hastings's app pinged. Chris read the message and related it to the room. "The vehicles are ready."

"All ready then? Come on, kids." Colin's announcement silenced the little rebels. They left the suite as planned. Well mostly.

Chris ignored the kids making faces on the elevator. His job was to protect the family from threats, not from each other.

A half hour after the private plane reached cruising altitude, Peter and Pollyanna fell asleep. Porter played a computer game with Colin. Chris opened his phone and saw a message he'd missed during the boarding process.

> Tian: Mom called. Dad had an episode. I am jump-seating to Boston on the 10 p.m. flight. Sorry to have missed you.

He leaned his head back against the seat and stared at the ceiling. The universe was not on his side.

The seat next to him squeaked softly. "I'd say a penny for your thoughts, but I am sure they're worth much more."

Chris turned his head to Candace's voice. "Nothing much. Cupid was off the mark this year."

"What do you mean? I thought you liked Tian."

"That's the problem. I like her, but we seem to be on two different flight paths. They aren't crossing often enough for us to take our relationship to the next level."

"Getting back a day early isn't going to help?"

"Her dad is ill. She'll be on a flight to Boston before we land." He leaned his head back against the seat to avoid Candace's gaze.

"When will she be back?"

"She's flying to Paris on the thirteenth and won't be back until the sixteenth. It's supposed to be her father's last flight."

"How long will you be apart?"

"Assuming I can see her on the sixteenth, thirteen days."

"Two weeks."

"And I've only known her for a month. I feel like there is so much potential for us."

"Something will work out."

"I keep thinking that. And then one of our jobs interferes." Trying to wipe the frustration from his mind, Chris ran a hand through his short hair. "It's crazy, the more time I spend with her, the more I think she could be the one. How insane is it that we live practically next door to each other and are having a long-distance relationship?"

"I haven't heard of that predicament before."

The hum of the engine filled the void in their conversation.

"I think she's going to dump me. Easier now than later, right?"

"She'd dump you over a job?"

"I said that out loud, didn't I? Let me rephrase. I think she is going to dump me because having a future together is so impossible. I traded around some days last time she was in Chicago so we could spend time together, but the truth is, neither of us are in a position to plan our schedules. She knows hers a month in advance, but all it takes is a blizzard to throw it off. My job can change at a moment's notice."

"That is one of the parts of my married life I like least—knowing that being spontaneous affects so many people. I can't decide

I want to go to a movie ten minutes before showing. Now that we've adopted the kids, it's even more true. I assume all parents have that problem. Mine is compounded because of security. I want to be fair to you guys too."

"Sorry. I shouldn't have said anything."

"I asked." Candace played with the ends of her scarf. "What if I could be spontaneous and help you?"

"What are you talking about?"

"I think Colin and I could use a few days of 'us' time. And the kids have so many parties next week, they won't miss us much..." Candace tapped her chin. "You have a passport, right?"

Chris's eyes narrowed. "Yes?"

"You sound unsure of that answer."

"I'm sure that I have a passport, I'm just not sure what you're proposing."

"I'm going to be spontaneous. If I help your Cupid in the process, so be it." Candace stood and walked to the front of the plane where her husband sat.

Chris spent the rest of the flight alternately trying to figure out what she meant and composing a long text to Tian.

> Chris: I hope you had a good flight and your father is better off than you expect. I'm trying not to be annoyed with the universe for keeping us apart. I already put in for the 17th off, but if you need to return to Boston with your father, I understand. I have this feeling that you're trying to end things with us. Please don't. I'm not fooling myself into thinking this will be easy. Our job schedules are going to need some fine tuning. Please give us a little longer.

In airplane mode the message couldn't go anywhere. He read the message again. It sounded too desperate. Chris hit delete.

Tian: Any social media video that claims jump seats are
     comfortable is lying. And backwards-facing landings
     are disconcerting.

Brit: You're jealous of my normal seat.

Simone: You're used to looking out windows when you land.
     How's your dad?

Tian: He says he is fine. Mom says no.

Brit: Hospital sent him home, so probably in the middle.

Tian: Why are you up anyway? It's 2 a.m.

Simone: I was watching Valentine's Day Hearthfire Channel
     movies. I need to go find a small town and a man in plaid.

Tian: I thought plaid was for Christmas.

Simone: It carries over. This one owns an organic farm.

Brit: I'd roll my eyes but I am too tired. Go to sleep. Especially
     you, Tian. I want the light off.

Tian turned off the light sitting on the nightstand in her old
bedroom. So much had changed over the years, but their shared
room hadn't. Boy band posters still littered Brit's side of the wall.
Tian needed sleep. Tomorrow would be full of phone calls. Who
knew what would be decided about Dad's last flight. He was
thinner. Other than that, she couldn't be sure. Everyone looks
tired at two in the morning. She checked her phone one last time,
hoping for a text from Chris. Still nothing.

Her alarm woke her sometime after sunrise. Tian hurried
to take a shower knowing whomever was last would get only
cold water. The bathroom door was locked. Brit beat her. Tian
stumbled back into the bedroom and turned on the light. Still
no message from Chris.

Tian: Are you back in Chicago?

Chris: Oh sorry. I wrote a long text on the airplane but
    didn't send it.

Tian: We need to talk.

Chris: The four words every man dreads.

Tian: I don't want to do this in a text.

Chris: Then don't.

Tian: I wish things were different. I can't ask you to change your
    job, and I don't know how to change mine. Now with my
    dad. I'll probably end up living here for half of my off time
    for the next six months.

Chris: Can we give us some time?

Tian: It will only hurt more.

Chris: It wouldn't hurt if we didn't care.

Tian's thumbs froze above her phone.

Tian: I know. But it still isn't fair to either of us.

Chris: Let's put this on hold until we can see each other.

Tian: That's 5 or 6 days at least.

Chris: I've asked for the 17th off. We can talk then.

Tian: K

Her phone rang.

"I'm not pressuring you into this. If you have decided you want to end things, I'll be cool with it." The warmth in his voice engulfed her like the hug she wished she could have.

"That's the problem. I don't want to, but I don't see a way forward either. Everything I think of ends up a dead end." A sob threatened to come out. Tian gulped it back and willed it to stay hidden. She needed to end this. "Promise me if we can't come up with a workable plan we will walk away?"

"How many plans have you been through?"

"Not that many. I can't ask you to leave your job, and my only option is to take a demotion so I can fly regional. Mrs. Ogilvie offered something, but I think it requires moving."

"You'd hate that."

"Pretty much. I could fly corporate, but that can be a messier schedule for the wrong company. Cargo is almost the same as now, only with more night flying."

"I could become an air marshal."

"You'd never be assigned to my plane. Even if you were, I would have to pretend not to know you."

"Tian!" Her mother called from downstairs.

"Mom needs me."

"I hope your dad is well enough for the flight."

"Thanks."

"Be safe."

The line went dead before she said goodbye. Probably his way of making sure she didn't say it for good.

Tian hurried down the stairs. Dad and Brit sat at the kitchen table. Tian couldn't remember the last time she'd had a meal with her family.

As soon as she sat down, her father said grace. Tian shared a wide-eyed look with Brit. Dad never prayed. She didn't know if he'd ever gone to church other than to get married.

Tian couldn't resist making a puddle with the maple syrup. "So what happened?"

"Only a little heart palpitation. Your mom overreacted."

"Are you cleared to fly?"

Dad frowned. "Not exactly. I am trying to work something out. This may be a four-pilot flight."

To her embarrassment, Tian's first thought was that if it was a four-pilot flight, they would divide the flight hours by four, and she'd be short on her qualification. She'd have to do more simulator time and try again to accumulate her consolidation hours.

"If I am a fourth," he added quickly, "I won't have any more responsibility than a glorified jump seater. But I'll be on the flight. I'll know later today."

"In the meantime, I have to take him down to get an echo."

Her father groaned.

"You know as well as I do HR wants it before they make their final decision. Girls, will you clean up? We should be back in a couple of hours."

After the last dish was done, Brit sat back down at the table. "If I didn't know better, I would think that this was a ploy for Dad to have us all together."

"Dad wouldn't risk not being able to fly."

"I have a feeling that whatever happened is more serious than either of them are saying. Hey, how are you getting back to Chicago for the flight?"

"I have a flight on the same commuter Dad does. As long as I sleep the night before, I'm good. I should get into Chicago three hours before the flight."

"You won't have your food for this trip."

"I am not taking frozen food to Paris. I should check on my flight."

Tian went up to their bedroom and opened her tablet. A notification for an email tagged as urgent caught her eye. The red exclamation point made her wonder as much as the words JOB OFFER.

She sat on her bed and opened the email, expecting spam.

Miss Christian Johnson—

> *Over the past week I've interviewed several pilots hoping to find the right fit for Robyn's Place Angel Flights. So far, I have only found two pilots for our team, both captains. One of them mentioned you might be a good fit*

for us. Having met you, I believe he is correct. Please find our offer attached, including benefits. I expect the position to start in June. The majority of the flights would be Monday, Tuesday, Friday, and Saturday with overnights only as needed. For the near future, we will be based out of Midway Airport.

Sincerely,

Candace Ogilvie

Chairman of the Board of Directors Robyn's Place

Tian read through the offer. If she had designed a dream job and hours, she couldn't have planned it better. Some weeks would be longer than others, depending on where the recipient families were, and the pay was more than she would make at Legacy with another five years' experience. Tempting to say the least. If she wanted to, she could stay on with Legacy as a reserve pilot, flying three or four days a month—enough to keep her at one hundred flight hours and advancing towards becoming a captain.

This couldn't be real, could it?

Nineteen

Convincing Simone to give him Tian's work schedule for the rest of the month required some heavy-duty bribes. Still unsure how he was going to convince Javier into taking Simone salsa dancing, Chris walked into Hastings Security knowing what he wanted. Hopefully, he could negotiate with whatever assignment Alan had called the meeting for.

"Thanks for coming in on your day off. Candace Ogilvie has requested you for two assignments. One is most unusual." Alan rubbed his jaw and stared at the computer screen.

Chris sat in the chair wondering what could be out of the ordinary enough that it had his boss puzzled.

"First, Candace has decided to surprise her husband with Valentine's Day in Paris. She specifically requested you to be part of her team, but only as airport and night building security. She is staying at her cousin Zoe Gooding's apartment, so there is already great security in place. They are using bodyguards fluent in French for the rest of the trip. I asked her why you, and she said there was no better bodyguard for the airport. They are flying commercial. I'm surprised they are leaving again so soon after Seattle. That's not their style."

"Or off of it completely." This must have been Candace's plan to put him in Paris at the same time as Tian. "If that's what she requested, I'll do it."

"But you've never done international before and don't speak French. I don't understand why she is insisting on you."

Chris shrugged. He didn't want to lie, and he didn't need to give Alan a reason to deny the request.

"The next request is somewhat expected. Robyn's Place needs security. Candace has been working on balancing security needs with a child-friendly atmosphere. Of course, Colin has been inventing systems to take care of much of the security while keeping it hidden including; cameras, and metal and chemical detectors, not to mention hidden medical equipment and health monitors. However, there is still a need for in-person security. Some people, like you, look the part, and other people like Dana, who remain incognito. Candace has been testing various members of our team by rotating them through shifts with her children. She wants you to be on the park security team. It's in the forma-tion stages."

"Would I need to move to Indiana?" The plan to build the park in a large Chicago area warehouse had been replaced with a larger park in connected custom buildings tripling the size of the original plan.

"Yes."

"May I think about it?"

Alan handed Chris a folder. "This is the basic plan. Still a work in progress."

"I thought it would be on a computer."

"ZoElle hasn't been feeling well the last few days, and I am a bit behind. I need to hire more support staff. If you know of anyone..."

"Not that I can think of. Is there anything else?"

"No."

"Then can I discuss my schedule? I'm willing to take all the weekends until the end of the month so I can schedule some days off." Chris pulled out Tian's schedule and traded his scheduled weekends off for a few other days.

Remarkably, everything fell into place for her father's final flight. As he predicted, he was flying in an observatory position. Both of the other pilots were captains leaving Tian conscious of her three-bar status and the only FO in the cockpit. Simone joined the crew and was assigned to business class where her mother flew with her grandfather. Brit sat with Tian's mother, also in business class. Chicago was experiencing one of those clear and cold February days that residents hated because of the windchill. Tian loved days like this for the view. The captain put her in the first officer's seat for takeoff, giving her more control than she would normally have in that position.

The takeoff was textbook perfect. The caption congratulated her before making his standard announcement to the passengers which wasn't so standard. "This is Captain Rochester. We have reached our cruising altitude of 32,000 feet. Before our Chicago-based cabin crew serves your meal, I have a special announcement. In the cockpit with me tonight is Captain Kurt Johnson on his final round trip flight as he is retiring. His daughter, First Officer Tian Johnson, is also flying with us as well. Sit back, relax, and enjoy the flight. Thank you for flying with Legacy Air. Next stop, Paris, France."

The captain turned off his microphone. "Now it's time for musical chairs. Kurt, you have been cleared to fly when we use autopilot. I know you will probably have that privilege again on our return trip. If you are feeling well enough, I would like to relinquish the controls to you."

Tian wasn't sure, but it seemed like Captain Rochester was choked up.

They switched places.

Tian's father was silent as he latched his seat belt and looked over the console. A wave of emotion slammed into her like a 70-knot crosswind. Captain Rochester waved the other captain out of the cockpit, leaving Tian alone with her father. She suspected they stood in the galley area just beyond the cockpit.

"Look at that world, Tian. From up here, we can't see the wars and strife, the loves and joys. From here, it is all peaceful. We are flying over millions of people who have no idea we are above their heads—and we have no thought for them. I'm going to miss this. There is so much I should have thought about but didn't in my life. Thank you for accepting my apology and flying with me this one last time."

"We will fly again in three days, won't we?"

"I don't think so. The captain shouldn't allow me to be alone in here with you as it is. We both know it. He is giving me five minutes for my last flight. The irony is I don't have to touch a single control."

"Thanks for arranging this." Tian forced the words past the lump in her throat.

"I hoped it would be more. I am so glad I didn't have a heart attack or something that would keep me from being in here at all."

They flew in silence for another minute before they were joined by Captain Rochester. "Captain Pitt is taking first rest. Kurt, you may leave or go as you wish. Tian, you take second, and I'll take third."

Most flights, Tian talked with the pilot at least some. For now, she relished the reverent silence that filled the cockpit.

"I think I'll go check out the bunks." Her father released his seat belt. He looked at Captain Rochester and something almost tangible passed between them.

The captain took his seat.

"Thank you for letting him have a moment with me."

"Back when I was a new pilot, I made a mistake. Nothing career ending, but enough to destroy my confidence. Your dad got me through it and back into the air. I owed it to him. I was standing outside the door. Your dad is a good man. I know people only see his relationship problems and judge him. He was so much more."

Tian cringed at the use of the past tense.

"I mean he is a good man."

"I know."

Someone knocked on the cockpit door. Tian checked the time. She took her headphones and tablet with her when she answered and switched places with Captain Pitt. Her father sat in one of the window seats of the small four-person lounge area adjacent to the crew's sleeping bunks.

"Have a minute?" he asked.

Tian sat across from him.

"Tell me what has been on your mind the last few days. It is more than this flight?"

"Not much. Chris. Our relationship isn't going to work. Not with our jobs. I received an ideal job offer flying four days a week for a charity to bring sick children to a specially designed theme park. The pay is amazing. According to the contract, they don't have a problem with me staying on part-time with Legacy to pick up a few more hours on a regional flight or two. But I'd be moving to Indiana which ruins any little chance we had of a relationship working."

"I am not sure what to tell you. Looking back, I made lots of mistakes with my life. In my heart, I knew some, or many, of my choices were selfish and wrong, but I didn't care. If I had followed my heart... I've already told you these things. What does your heart say?"

"I want to take this job. While it blows any chance I might have had with Chris, it gives me a chance to have a family and be home almost every night and still fly."

"Then take it."

"What about Chris?"

"You've only known him a few weeks, are you that invested in him?"

"Oddly, yes. Which is so weird because, as you pointed out, we haven't had much time together. I want it all—the perfect job *and* Chris."

"You deserve it all."

"If only, right?"

"Don't go there." Her father sighed in frustration. "There could be a path you don't see yet."

"Maybe. I should get my rest."

Tian climbed into the bunk and fastened the seat belt across her waist. She put on her earbuds and turned on her relax mix. She fell into a light sleep. In her dreams, she flew Candace's dream flights meeting child after child, giving them a week or a few days away from their hospitals. So different than flying entitled passengers from one vacation to another or business people to another meeting. A noble purpose making the world better one child at a time. She'd never considered that part of her discontent was the need to do something that mattered until the opportunity had presented itself.

She woke fifteen minutes before she needed to be back in the cockpit. She went to the restroom. Her father was no longer in the lounge. She opened her mail app and composed an email to send when she landed.

> *Mrs. Ogilvie—*
>
> *I am very interested in your offer. I have a few questions. Is there a time we can talk? I'll be back in the States on the 17th.*
>
> *Christian (Tian) Johnson*

Now if she could solve her relationship problems so easily.

Twenty

THE PASTRIES IN THE WINDOW looked and smelled amazing.
Chris went inside the bakery and ordered using gestures. The
chocolate croissant tasted as good as it smelled. He continued
to the address Simone had texted.

Brit and Simone sat in the lobby with an older man Chris
assumed was Tian's father. "Thanks for meeting me."

"I can't believe you're here. Tian's taking a nap." Simone yawned.
"Which is where I want to be."

Chris handed them papers printed with QR codes. "Just scan
these, and they will give you a Paris tour pass. Can you have Tian
at the dock at 1630—I mean 4:30 this afternoon?"

"She'll be there," said Brit.

Both women stood and left.

"Stay. I assume you know who I am."

"Tian's father. I'm glad you could make your flight."

"Me too." His breathing became more labored. "I need to rest,
so no beating around the bush. You mean something to my girl—
her mom says, more than any other man has. I'm not sure how
you two can work it out, but you better try or I will haunt you."

"We are trying."

"Try harder." Mr. Johnson closed his eyes. "Would you mind escorting me to my room?"

Chris walked back to his own lodgings, not paying attention to the architecture or the sites. Tian was right, their careers were going to be in the way. And if he took the offered job, even more in the way. He was torn. He liked kids and working with Candace at her outreaches at the schools and children's hospitals. From the outline he was given, he'd also have an opportunity to plan much of the security.

He could turn it down. His position with Hastings wouldn't change. Tian need not know he gave up a promotion for her; she was worth it.

"Come on, Tian." Simone stood next to Brit in the doorway.

"But Dad—"

Tian's mother crossed her arms. "I'm staying with him. Go."

"But—"

"You have two days in Paris. These passes will let us take a peek at some of the sites. You can't miss this."

"Go, or I'll write you out of my will." Dad's voice was weak but firm.

Tian threw on her jacket. "Fine, I am going."

Brit rushed them to catch a hop-on-hop-off tour bus which took them to the other side of the Seine and the Eiffel Tower. The line to go up snaked around part of the park. An attendant informed them that without a specific appointment, their wait was likely to be more than three hours.

"This must be the most sought-after Valentine's spot in the city." Brit opened her phone app. "There's a boat tour on the Seine. We should take that."

"I loved those in the old movies. Cary Grant and Audrey Hepburn took a dinner cruise in one. It looked so cool." Simone did a little twirl more reminiscent of another Audrey Hepburn movie.

"I don't think this has any food, but it would be a fun way to tour and see lots of things." Now that she was out of the hotel, Tian's eagerness to see the city increased.

"Maybe we can find a crepe cart on the way." Brit gestured to the street they should take to get to the river and the dock.

Nutella tasted better in Paris. Tian wiped the last of the hazelnut-chocolate spread from her fingers. They neared the point of departure. The line was only thirty people or so long. They joined it and waited for the next boat.

"Tian, will you hold our places? I need to find a restroom."

Before her sister and cousin returned, the line moved forward.

Tian: They are boarding.

Brit: In a second. Save us some seats.

She found three seats next to a huge window and claimed them by laying her jacket across two of the plastic seats next to her. Staring across the water, she wondered which buildings were significant. The engines of the boat rumbled. Tian looked around. They were leaving. Where were Brit and Simone? They had to be on the boat. She stood searching the back of the viewing room. The door behind her opened.

"Excuse me, are you saving this seat?"

That voice. It couldn't be. She whirled around, nearly bumping into Chris. He braced her by the elbows. "Surprise."

"What are you doing here?"

"Happy Valentine's Day."

Truth? It had just gotten a whole lot happier. "How…?"

Chris sat and pulled her down next to him. "Candace arranged this."

"What? Why?"

"Best guess is she enjoys playing Cupid."

"I can't believe you're here." She placed her palm in the center of his chest and felt his heart beating.

His chuckle rumbled through her. "I guarantee you are not hallucinating."

"How did you get here? When?" She would have noticed if Chris showed up on the manifest.

"I flew with the Ogilvies on a different carrier. I didn't want you to be distracted."

"This is crazy. How did you have vacation so quickly?"

"I didn't. This is a working trip. However, I am only on active duty on the plane. The rest of the time, I am the on-call reserve."

The boat slowed, coming into another stop. "Brit, Simone. I forgot about them. They're lost."

"Oh, I was supposed to tell you not to worry about them. They will find alternate transportation back to the hotel."

"They were in on this?"

"Your mother and father know too."

The boat docked. Chris took Tian's hand. "Come on. Our dinner awaits. Unless you have something in your suitcase you'd rather eat."

"Are you kidding? This is Paris. I am not eating one of my frozen meals when I can have a croissant with marmalade or a crepe from a corner vendor."

A car awaited them in an area beyond the dock. "A car?"

"Candace's cousin knew someone…I've never seen anyone so excited to plan a date as Candace was."

"She planned this?" A chauffeur opened the door. Tian looked down at her jeans. She wasn't dressed for anything fancy.

"It was a fifty-fifty split. Which reminds me, do you have any food allergies? The friend suggested a dinner to order."

"No allergies." The interior of the car was everything one would expect from the French equivalent of a limo. "I feel so under-dressed."

"The friend—her name is Gina—told me this place was not dressy. Your jeans and sweater will be great. I was hoping for the Eiffel Tower, but even with their connections there was no way."

They stopped at a little café. The chauffeur held the door for them. "Tell them Gina sent you."

Chris nodded. Inside they were led to a corner table. A single red rose lay across her plate.

"Your idea?" Tian brought it to her nose.

"I wanted more, but Candace pointed out you were flying back, and customs didn't like fresh flowers."

"Oh, Chris. You've gone to so much trouble. I feel so bad. Instead of coming up with a plan to keep us together, I've taken a job that will take me away from Chicago." Tears formed in her eyes.

Chris's heart sank. Everything had been going according to plan, but now this? "What job?"

"With Mrs. Ogilvie's charity. I'll be flying the planes. I haven't signed anything." She wiped away a tear. "I can turn it down. We are more important."

He held her hand. "Sign. This is the best news I've had in days."

Tian's eyes opened wide.

"What do you mean?"

"Alan offered me a job as the head of security for the amusement park. I was going to turn it down because it meant I had to leave Chicago and any chance I had for a relationship with you."

Tian took a deep breath and sat back in her chair. "I don't believe it."

Someone served their dinners. At that point, Chris could have eaten three-day-old fast food and not known the difference. All his focus was on Tian.

Over a dessert which contained chocolate, Tian posed the question, "What if we don't work out? We will have both moved…"

"Are you taking the job to be with me?"

"No. You were the only reason I hesitated to take it."

"Same for me. We don't have to move until late May. That gives us plenty of time to figure out if what we have is —" He wasn't ready to say the word yet.

Tian supplied it. "Love?"

"Lasting love." The small table between them was too much. He lifted Tian's hand to his lips, the only thing he could kiss without making a scene. "I know how I feel about you. I may have thought I was in love before, but my desire to be with you, even if all we do is talk over a table, is overwhelming."

"In those quiet moments when I'm flying, I find myself thinking mostly of you. I've been driving myself crazy trying to figure out how to continue being us."

The waiter reappeared. "They paid your bill in advance and instructed me to give you this."

As soon as the waiter left Chris unfolded the paper.

"What is it?"

"A map. It says 'Recommended route for a stroll.' If it's raining or you're tired, call this number for a car." He handed the paper to Tian.

"Do you know where this takes us?"

"Not really." He didn't care as long as he was with her. Even if it was the catacombs which didn't sound remotely romantic.

"To the bridge with all the locks."

"What are you talking about?"

Tian scooted her chair back. "I'll tell you on the way."

A few meters from the restaurant stood a stone archway in front of a park. Chris scanned it for any sight of danger before pulling Tian into the shadow and the kiss he'd waited to give her for days. A kiss of promise, lingering and slow. Although he hoped she would understand what he was trying to express, he ended the kiss to whisper the words. "I love you."

Tian didn't answer with words. Instead, she pulled him back into a kiss more passionate than the first. Reluctantly, he allowed the kiss to end when she pulled back.

"I love you too. Be my valentine?" she asked.

"Forever."

Epilogue

Annoyed at the last-minute call, Chris hurried to the Hastings gym. Tian had been understanding about pushing tonight's date back an hour, as had his brother-in-law when he'd called the restaurant. The ring box, safely placed in the zippered interior pocket of his jacket, sat just above his heart.

ZoElle stood at the door with a Hastings t-shirt pulled tightly over her expanding belly.

"Do you know what's going on?" he asked.

ZoElle smiled. "They need your help for a few moments. Gear up."

Only the lights over the sparring mat were on.

Abbie stood in the center of the room. Other people, probably students, sat on the benches that bordered the gym.

"Thanks for coming. Alex was going to help me, but he got called out because of some St. Patrick's Day thing. Anyway, you know the drill. Your goal is the purse."

He raised his eyebrows. She had to be kidding. Abbie smiled. Chris turned to the wall of safety gear. He took off his jacket, set it on the shelf and put on the head protection.

"Ready?" asked Abbie.

"Yes."

"Begin."

Hoping for a different outcome than the last time he'd sparred with Abbie, he turned and stepped into his attack. Only it wasn't Abbie, with the bag slung over her shoulder. It was Tian. Already on his second step, he faltered.

"Get the bag," ordered Abbie.

As he had with Abbie a couple of months ago, he reached for the bag. Tian's arm shot up, and he was on his back, looking at the ceiling.

Tian leaned over. "Are you okay?"

"I've fallen for you."

Laughter filled the room. Chris turned his head and recognized the students in the shadows as his fellow Hastings team members and Tian's roommates. The Ogilives were also there. Two could play at this game. He rolled to his feet and took off the safety gear and put back on his jacket. Tian still stood on the mat, accepting a hug from Abbie.

Chris dropped to one knee. "Tian, I have fallen for you in more than one way."

The chatting in the room died instantly. Tian stood with her right hand over her mouth. Abbie gave her a gentle push forward. Chris clasped her left hand. And pulled the ring box out of his pocket.

"Christian Rae Johnson, will you marry me?"

TWO WEEKS LATER.

The county clerk handed the clipboard back to Tian. "I asked for your information, not his."

"That *is* my information."

"But—" The clerk looked from one form to the other.

Chris leaned forward in his chair. "Our drivers licenses should clear this up."

The clerk held both licenses at eye level, comparing the photos with their faces. "You have the same name?" He lowered the cards. "How do you tell yourselves apart?"

The man shook his head as if ridding his mind of a trance. "Sorry, stupid question. Of course, you can tell yourselves apart. In all my years working here, I've never seen a couple with the same name."

"Our middle names are spelled differently." Tian pointed out the difference that needed to be clear on the license.

Chris squeezed her hand. "That is how we knew which one of us was called to jury duty."

The clerk looked at his monitor. "So if someone does the Brangelina thing with your name, it comes out as Christian, which is your name."

Tian and Chris exchanged a look. "It's better than Tiris."

"No one will believe this at the convention." The clerk laughed with them.

"I'm more worried about the IRS questioning our joint tax return," said Chris.

"On the bright side, I don't have to worry about changing my passport or anything else."

The clerk looked up. "That is a bonus. However, I am seeing more and more marriages where one spouse doesn't take the other's name."

"I thought about it briefly, but hyphenated Johnson-Johnson feels too corporate." Tian couldn't stop grinning not from the conversation, which was funny, but from the fact in just three days she'd be Mrs. Christian R. Johnson.

The clerk laughed at Tian's joke. He turned to his printer and pulled off a paper. "There you go. One wedding license. Best wishes and good luck."

Chris took Tian's hand as they left the office. "Are you sure you're ready for this?"

Tian turned to face him. "Yes. I want to spend the rest of my life confusing people with our names." She placed a hand on his shoulder and brushed a soft kiss across his lips. "They should take bets on who we can confuse most. My bet is on the nurse who helps us fill out the birth certificate for our first child."

Child? Chris loved the idea. "No, the first kindergarten teacher when our son insists his parents have the same name."

"Son? You mean daughter?"

"I guess we'll need to make sure to have one of both." Chris dropped a kiss on her lips and ignored the people passing by.

The End

Acknowledgements

I GREW UP WITH MY grandfather telling airline stories at the dinner table every time he visited. Grandpa Pitt worked for Western Airlines from 1938 – 1972 and convinced me it was the "Only way to fly." His stories sparked the idea to have a multigenerational family of aviators.

Special thanks to the real Captain Andrew and his wife for their expertise. Any mistakes regarding pilots, planes, or the aviation industry are mine not theirs.

As always, thanks to Tammy and Nanette who are so willing to help make all my projects better. I would never make it through a day without Cindy whose texts and messages keep me writing.

Big thanks to Maria for the excellent edits, and to Dallin for his first journey as a proofreader. Neither are not to be blamed for any remaining errors. Thank you all!

My family, for sharing their home with the fictional characters who often get fed better than they did. Seriously, I haven't cooked in a year. And my husband, who encourages me every crazy step of the way.

And to my Father in Heaven for putting these wonderful people, and any I may have forgotten to mention, in my life. I am grateful for every experience and blessing I have been granted.

About the Author

Lorin Grace was born in Colorado and has been moving around the country ever since, living in eight states and several imaginary worlds. She holds a degree in graphic design which comes in handy with creating book covers. Currently, she lives with her husband, and a dog who is insanely jealous of her laptop.

When not writing, Lorin enjoys creating graphics, visiting historical sites, museums, painting furniture, and reading. Three of her books, her debut novel, *Waking Lucy* (2017), *Mending Fences* (2018), and *Not the Bodyguard's Baby* (2020) have won Recommend Read awards in the League of Utah Writers Published book contest.